To the girls who want to fly

when all they can do is walk.

Contents

—————))-▾-((—————

HINDSIGHT

16th May 1998

Coimbatore, India

Karuna Institute of Technology

The car screeched and careened its way to G.K.N.M. Hospital on Netaji Road. Sandhya lay unconscious on the back seat. Blood seeped from cuts on her shoulder and back, staining her kurta and salwar making patterns that in other times would have been fascinating to watch. Her hair was tousled, her braids undone. Dirt marks ran the length of her body.

They arrived in a squeal of brakes and, waiting men bore her to a private ward. Efficient nurses buzzed around in their gowns and cap, taking vital readings, undressing her, and covering her with the green hospital gown. A wiry middle-aged woman, with silver white hair and a spotless white coat, walked in purposefully and began her examination with slow, steady, gloved hands. Her low but sharp voice dictated medical terms in a monotone as a nurse on her right kept notes in a neat hand. She left with the same efficiency with which she had entered.

"Report fax panna solliten. Nee kavalai padadhe."

(I have asked them to fax the report. Do not worry.)

She addressed a lean, athletic young man who had been instrumental in bringing Sandhya there. His forehead creased and straightened in the way of someone coming to a decision.

She hoped her reassurance would be enough for this man, the nephew she loved as dearly as her child.

"Athe, unga help marakka maaten. Sandhya inga irrukatum. Vennila irrupa naan thirumba vara varayum."

(Aunt, I will not forget your help. Let Sandhya be here. Veninila will be here until I return)

Surya left, thanking his aunt profusely. Inside the room, Sandhya stirred but did not wake. Vennila sat by her side, holding her hand, silent tears marking a path from her eyes to the floor.

———

SAVITHRI AND JAYARAMAN:

THE NEWS AND MEMORIES

December 17, 2012

Chennai, India

The cyclists weave in and out of the chaotic T. Nagar traffic. It is 6:30 am. Hardly a time one associates with chaos. Jayaraman walks along the side of the road, stepping over slushy puddles, animal excrement and decaying matter. He has a newspaper tucked under his arm and a cloth bag with fresh vegetables from the corner market. A pair of reading glasses peek from a white shirt with almost invisible brown stripes running vertically down. His veshti is folded up and tied across his waist. He loves his early morning walk surrounded by the people of his city, the dust, and the humidity. He misses them sorely on his yearly sojourns to his daughter Usha's home in the Silicon Valley.

Jayaraman's grandson Ishaan is older now. Jayaraman and Savithri's visits to the US had begun when Ishaan had been born. He had tagged along initially merely to accompany Savithri as she tended to their daughter Usha and grandchild Ishaan.

Jayaraman had been bored out of his wits until his son-in-law had gifted him with a laptop. He had taken to technology quickly for someone of his age. He had loved the fast internet in the US, often emailing Sandhya and enjoying her repartee. A smile forms at the thought of Sandhya. They say parents do not have favorites. He does and his is

Sandhya, his youngest daughter. Usha had been born a wise old soul. He did not remember her demanding attention as a child or later as a teenager. Sandhya had been a handful, commanding and grabbing his attention with both her hands. She had had him besotted from the moment she had been born.

One of his favorite memories from his daughters' childhood had been pulling into their home on his motorbike and looking into the hall window to see Sandhya's smiling face pressed against the bars. He would walk quickly, knowing she would fling the door open and rush into his arms. She would ask, "What have you brought for me?" Each day he would pick something from his office. A spare sheet of paper, a gem clip, a stapler. Sometimes he would stop at the grocers on his way home, remembering to pick up a Cadbury's lollipop for both girls.

As Sandhya had grown and blossomed into a woman, her attentions had turned towards friends. He had been disappointed, masking his sadness with silence. Savithri and Sandhya had been at loggerheads all through her teenage years. "Those books will be the end of her," Savithri had predicted, not realizing how much those words would come back to haunt her.

If Usha had flitted through high school, amidst her clique of socially vociferous girls, Sandhya had taken to books with a vengeance. He had often woken at night to get a tumbler of water only to find Sandhya reading under the bulb in the kitchen, doors closed. He would tuck her in, pretending to worry she would be late for school, while secretly admiring her passion for the written word.

He had watched her debate with her friends, handle phone transactions in English and talk to strangers with consummate ease, her command over the language intimidating him and others.

When she had been accepted at Karuna Institute of Technology in Coimbatore, he had been crestfallen. She had been ecstatic at the thought of leaving home. "I am going to fly far, far away Appa," she had said with a sparkle in her eyes making circles around him, arms outstretched, like a bird would.

Before his mind can go to places he does not want it to go, he shakes himself and quickens his pace, knowing Sandhya will call as she makes her tea each evening. He looked forward to the daily ritual, waiting patiently for Savithri to hand the phone over to him. They discussed world affairs, gossip, her work day and, his day. She missed the physicality of newspapers and lived vicariously through his words.

They used to have newspapers delivered a long while ago, but with their frequent visits overseas, they had fallen into a different pattern, buying the paper and vegetables fresh each day. Now, that he is retired, this ritual offers him a chance to get out of the house and be alone with his thoughts. He and Savithri will have been married 42 years this year. He had provided for the family materially and she had, emotionally. They took pride in their two daughters and the families they were now building.

Reaching home, he notices Savithri standing at the door as if waiting for his arrival. Something about the set of her face bothers him.

Wordlessly, she takes the bag and paper from his hands and takes them to the dining table that also serves as a place to cut vegetables and catch up on newspapers and magazines. The TV is on, unusually. Raising his eyebrows, Jayaraman settles in the sofa. A second cup of coffee materializes in front of him before Savithri seats herself by the phone on the other sofa.

"... is critical and doctors are horrified by the extent of the injuries. Police have questioned the man who was with her..."

"... all but one of the assaulters have been apprehended..."

Jayaraman spends the next few minutes hearing the details of a horrific rape in New Delhi being played out sensationally on TV. Wordlessly he reaches for The Hindu and reads the rest. His stomach feels unsettled and a thin skin forms on the top of his coffee as it cools.

———

Fourteen years earlier, as he had been waiting for Sandhya to let him know she had vacated the hostel to catch the train to Madras, he had received a call from her college. A bland voice over the phone had told him that his daughter had been in an accident and was at the hospital. Before he could gather what had happened, they had hung up. With no number to call back and no contact person, he had done what a panicked father would do.

The taxi they had hired had sped through the darkness along NH 47 to Coimbatore. They had arrived in the early hours of dawn, having stopped only once for a toilet break. Reaching the college, they had been redirected to G.K.N.M, Hospital.

The peon who had been the only person in the admin offices had said he had no other information. They had rushed, tired, their stomachs in knots. Savithri had not said one word since they had left.

Seeing Sandhya in a hospital gown, an IV line running to her arms, bandages on her head and neck had hit them both physically. Savithri had let out a strangled cry and rushed to Sandhya. He had grasped the door for support. A girl—he had later learned her name was Vennila—had supported him and escorted him to a chair.

They had learned from the girl and the doctor on duty that their Sandhya had been assaulted by a bunch of college boys in the stadium at about 7:30 pm the night before. Sandhya had a head injury and other physical wounds that would heal. "It was not rape," the lady had insisted. The more they stressed on it, the more he feared it had been.

There had been the boy, Surya, whose face had been ravaged by a grief mirroring his own. He had said little. It turned out he had been the one to find her and bring her to the hospital. Jayaraman had clasped his hands in his own and wept with gratitude. It had broken him to see Sandhya like that. She had been accepted to Villanova, a visa interview scheduled for the following week, and here she had lain, mute, having survived something unspeakable.

He had not said anything when she had opened her eyes and looked at him. Instead, he had held her close, rocking back and forth when she had cried. He had not left her side since. "Appa, why did they do this to me?" she had asked, her anguish scarring him more than the sight of her wounds.

Over the next few days, he had gathered from the nurse and Vennila that the perpetrators were related to the college principal and around these parts, they carried clout with the police and lawmakers as well.

"You can file a complaint, Uncle," Surya had said, looking him in the eye, his arm in a cast. "Nothing will happen. They will spoil her reputation and ruin any chances she has of putting this behind her."

"What should I do?" he had asked, wringing his hands, and feeling helpless about his middle-class roots and absolute lack of connections. "Naan paathukaren saar. Neenga Sandhya va paathukanga."

He had held on to those words ringing mildly of a promise of justice, like a lifeline, a promise. They had left for Madras as soon as Sandhya had been discharged from the hospital. Sandhya had leaned on him watching as Surya loaded the car trunk will all the traces of her life in Coimbatore. Surya and Vennila had stayed with them until they left, tearfully waving bye. Emotions, memories and hopes, all left behind in the dry Coimbatore air, trapped for perpetuity.

Savithri's voice drags him back to the present. "I worry about Sandhya. If she hears or reads the news, it will make her relive everything."

Her voice is placid, concealing undercurrents of helplessness and anxiety. He reaches for her hand, holding it for a bit, before letting go.

———————

VENNILA: GHOSTS FROM THE PAST

17 December, 2012 - Evening

Sirumugai, Tamil Nadu

Sirumugai is a small village on the banks of the Bhavani River. Four miles away is the town of Mettupalayam. About an hour away is the city of Coimbatore. Buses ply along Sirumugai, dropping off weary, home-bound residents. Strangers are unusual in these parts.

It is idyllic, with panoramic views of the Nilgiri mountain ranges and coconut trees swaying in the breeze. Lush banana plantations dot the landscape and the air is filled with birdsong.

A big concrete compound hides the house from view. Wrought iron gates open to a dirt path that leads to the front portico. Flowering trees and bushes are planted along the periphery and the air is rich with the smells of jasmine and plumeria. Unseen snakes slither in the woods beyond the house.

It is the kind of place where sunset brings a grinding halt to all activity. Children are called home and the smells of freshly-made dinner waft through open kitchen windows. The TV is on and the ceiling fans are set on low speed. The odd mosquito buzzes by before being felled by a swatting hand.

Vennila is in the kitchen, grinding masala for the kurma. Her house help, Rani, is sitting by her side on the floor, scraping coconut with an iron aruvamanai. Thirteen-year-old Shyam is outside, playing cricket with his friends. A mix of sounds percolates into the kitchen— the odd vehicle passing the house, the crickets on the fence at the rear of the house, stray dogs barking around the corner. The Sun TV anchor declares that it is time for headline news.

Surya should be home any minute now, thinks Vennila. The aapam batter is ready, pure white with air bubbles. It smells of yeast and coconut milk. Vennila transfers the masala to the bowl, rinses the mixer attachment and steps into the hallway.

"Shyam! Come inside and wash up. Appa will be here soon and it is your math exam tomorrow. One more week, chellam, and then you can play as much as you want."

She smiles indulgently as he walks in, sulking at having had to stop halfway through an interesting game of cricket, and disappears into the bathroom to wash up. She is about to head back into the kitchen when Surya's car pulls up in front of the house. The driver opens the rear passenger door and Surya steps out in his immaculate white linen shirt and relaxed trousers. He looks exhausted. She meets him at the door and takes the briefcase from his hand. He removes his glasses and sets them on the side table before sinking into the sofa.

"Can I get a cup of coffee? I have a headache," he says. Vennila looks at him with concern and hurries inside to brew a cup.

"...*today in Delhi, the accused perpetrators of the Nirbhaya rape were apprehended...*"

Surya turns the volume up on the TV and leans in to listen. He is sitting there with a blank look on his face when Vennila returns a few minutes later with a steaming cup of coffee. She places the steel davara and tumbler on the table in front of him as well as a plate of murukku.

"Are you okay?" she asks, touching his forehead lightly for signs of fever. He does not reply, so she turns her attention to the TV where the newscaster is interviewing someone.

"... *She is a bright girl. Always enjoyed school... We moved from the village to Delhi so she could go to college...*"

Vennila sits next to Surya, her hands seeking his as they watch the outrage unfold on screen. Shyam joins them, a math sample paper in hand, seating himself across from them.

"Enna aachu, Amma? Why is everyone crying?" Shyam's voice breaks his parents' reverie and Surya switches the TV off and takes a sip of the coffee.

"Onnumille, kanna. You go in and study. We will have dinner shortly." Vennila gently maneuvers Shyam out of the room. She stands behind Surya, pressing his temples. Words do not seem necessary.

Dinner is a quiet affair. Vennila serves her son and husband first and joins them as they eat. "This is good!" says Shyam. Vennila serves him another aapam and ladles the kurma on his plate. As they finish and Vennila clears the table, Surya surprises her by announcing that he is going for a walk. There is no invitation for her to join him. She sighs and nods, knowing why. She herself would not mind taking a walk around their colony of homes to sort her thoughts in peace.

After settling Shyam at the dining table with his books and sample paper, she sits across him with her laptop, scanning the news of the day. She clicks on the headline about the Delhi rape, reading clinically, dispassionately, as if connecting with the event will bring to the fore everything she has been suppressing. On an impulse she logs into Facebook and searches for Sandhya Jayaraman. A few hits come up, none of them even remotely like the Sandhya who had once been her best friend. She smiles wryly and searches for Aditya Raghavan. This time she finds the Aditya she is looking for. She scans through his sparse friends' list, looking for Sandhya. Not finding her, she gives up and closes the laptop.

She leans back and watches Shyam duel with his questions. Eyes furrowed, the back of the pencil in his chin, he is lost to the world around him. Her Shyam, named for Sandhya, harbinger of dusk. The twilight zone between day and night where the lines blur.

Fourteen years. That is how long it has been since she had last seen Sandhya or heard from her. They had hugged as friends did and Sandhya had gotten into a car with her parents, her bags stowed in the trunk, and driven away. No promises to keep in touch. No contact numbers. Just a sad little smile as if ruing what had come to be. Vennila had walked back to the car where Surya was waiting and they had gone on with their lives.

———

They had met for the first time in the summer of 1993, in college. Sandhya was from Madras. A pleasant-faced, well dressed girl who had

had sat next to her during orientation. They had introduced themselves and walked to their first class together. They had sat next to each other at their first class and every class thereafter.

Their friendship had not been premeditated. They had fallen into it and found no reason to expand their cozy circle. They had shared an interest in books although Sandhya read voraciously and Vennila did not. They liked to have long conversations on friendship, on women's rights, on pursuing a career after college. Conversations that meandered and had no finite end point.

Unlike most of the girls Vennila had been friends with at school, Sandhya did not talk about boys, love, or marriage. Not that she was not interested. She had often seen Sandhya look at this boy, Aditya, a computer science major from her old school, wistfully. Sandhya had never really sought him out but there was something about the way she looked at him that Vennila recognized. She often saw that in herself when she looked at Surya.

Surya and Vennila were related and it was a foregone conclusion for their families that they would one day marry each other. Neither of them had set store by it growing up, often teasing each other about it. Surya would often tell her that she was free to pursue other men and that he had his sights set on a few other girls. They would laugh and wish each other well. They had an easy companionship unmarred by the expectations that their families had of them.

———————

Vennila had lived with her parents in R.S. Puram, an affluent part of Coimbatore. She had gone to Kikani, a co-ed school with an emphasis on speaking English. Surya had finished school at SIV, the only school of repute in Sirumugai, intent on taking over his father's business right after. Her uncle had stood his ground—Surya had to have a college education before he could start working with him. Vennila had been admitted to Karuna Institute of Technology to study electronic and electrical engineering. It made sense that Surya would follow where she went, even if it meant paying a huge capitation fee, that his father could thankfully afford. Thus, the informally betrothed relatives and Sandhya had become a group. They ate lunch together and spent most of their breaks sitting under the trees by the stadium, trading gossip, sharing stories about their families and becoming a clique unto themselves.

Somewhere in their second year, Vennila had known something had changed. It had happened gradually. Some days she would walk into their classroom a few minutes before class and find Sandhya and Surya deep in conversation. They would make space for her to join, and yet she would feel like an intruder. They mostly talked about business and how women do not really aspire to much.

Sandhya would be spirited, her black eyes dancing with conviction as she talked about her dreams to be an entrepreneur and to shatter glass ceilings. Surya would put her down ever so gently, reminding her that marriage beckoned and her decisions would not be hers alone. She would scoff and swear she would find someone who would carve space for her in his life.

It was not the conversations themselves that affected Vennila. She saw hunger in Surya's eyes when he looked at Sandhya. She saw hunger in Surya's eyes when he looked at Sandhya. For the first time in her life,

Vennila realized she had been in love with Surya for over half her life. She did not know if Sandhya realized it or not, and their friendship came in the way of her saying anything.

So she had watched as the two had moved increasingly closer. The pull they shared had been magnetic, she was swept along with the tides that carried them. Aditya had been an infrequent presence in their lives, stopping occasionally to talk to Sandhya ostensibly to exchange books. She felt a kinship with him, a bond born from unrequited love.

Things had come to a head at the beginning of their last year together when in a heated moment, Vennila had forced the issue. Both Surya and Sandhya had been quick to deny they had feelings for each other. They had cooled, kept their distance. Yet their chemistry scorched anyone within standing distance of them. Vennila had stepped back, asked for a different lab partner, and mulled a life sans Surya.

Then it had happened. Sandhya had her admit for a Masters in Computer Science from Villanova University in Pennsylvania, USA. She was ecstatic and Surya despondent. They danced around their feelings, alienating everyone around them. The last day of college, they had met as a group, the three of them, relived their four years of college, exchanged cards, signed yearbooks, and said their byes. They had walked to the bus stop, Vennila ahead and Sandhya and Surya behind. Laughing, she had turned to point something out to them and fallen silent when she saw linked hands and a conversation that needed no words. She had walked ahead in a blinding haze of rage and envy and stopped only when she reached the petty shop by the gate. Surya had run behind her, shame writ large on his face. Sandhya was nowhere to be seen.

"Sandhya dropped the book Aditya had given her near the trees. She said she will get it and join us in a bit," Surya had said. He had also held Vennila's hands as he had confessed how he really felt about Sandhya. About how he knew he would never have the guts to let her know. He had poured it all out, a gush of tormented emotions encompassing a misguided sense of duty towards his family, to Vennila and what society would make of him. He had reached out to take her other hand, to apologize, when a junior had run to them, muttering something about Sandhya being hurt. He had listened and Vennila had seen blood drain from his face.

Then he had taken off, running back the way he had come. Vennila had hesitated, then followed him. They had arrived within minutes of each other at a scene that seemed unreal. The sirens of approaching campus security, a clutch of men running pell-mell and an air of devastation. A lone figure sitting on the ground, holding an unconscious woman, her clothes torn, gashes on her face and blood seeping from her head and near her knees. Her hair was undone, her kurta ripped and her salwar torn. Surya had dropped to his knees, a guttural cry emanating from him. Aditya had been holding Sandhya's head on his chest, his face shocked.

Vennila had taken charge, rousing Surya from his grief, reminding him that he needed to get help for Sandhya. They had worked as a team, calling his aunt, summoning an ambulance and leaving Aditya with instructions to handle the campus staff. It had not been long after that Sandhya had left their lives and never turned back.

Vennila looked at the clock and the empty hallway and roused herself to send Shyam to bed. Surya would be a long time coming and she had a long night ahead.

———————

SURYA: TRIP DOWN MEMORY LANE

The voice of the TV anchor echoes in Surya's head as he walks along the pavement that leads past his house to the nearby park. Surya is a man of few words. When emotions threaten to overwhelm him, he prefers to walk, letting the physical act of putting step ahead of step soothe him into a state where he can examine his thoughts without emotions clouding his judgment. What he has just seen on TV has taken him years back, yet not a day has gone past when the image of Sandhya, broken and battered, has not crossed his mind, either in sleep or in wakefulness. He has learned to function despite that, shoving the images to the back of his head where he can process them at his own time and pace. Today, the memories descend on him as if the dam holding them back has broken, leaving in its wake debris and destruction.

He remembers the first time he had seen her in the canteen, buying something while Vennila waited for her at a table. She had possessed an innate grace that had set her apart in the crowd he was used to. She had walked back, two plates of bajjis and two coffees precariously placed on a lop-sided tray. He had rushed to help her and her voice as she had thanked him had sounded musical. He was not someone who believed in love or love at first sight. Yet, if he had to go back and pick the moment he had fallen in love, it had to be that.

They had become friends, with Vennila serving as buffer. They had kept their conversations flippant, their interactions platonic. Two years had gone by when things had changed. He had come to class early one morning, driving straight from the nearby town after his dad had needed him to take a machine part to Coimbatore to be fixed. He had stayed the night at the workshop with the mechanic and driven back in the morning with the repairs done.

He had walked into what he had thought was an empty classroom only to find Sandhya deeply immersed in a book. He had seen her eyes tracking each line, her lips forming the words as she swirled through the pages into another era. He had sat by the window and watched as she turned the pages of Pride and Prejudice, her face mirroring what she felt. A gamut of emotions had run across her face and when she had laughed out loud at something, he had not been able to resist joining her. She had jumped, alarm writ large on her face as she realized she had company.

He had apologized and they had talked about the story she had been reading. She had told him that she loved the early mornings when the class was empty. The hostel never afforded her this kind of peace, she had said. She had been wistful, eyes looking beyond the walls, her mind trapped in a world far away when she had drawn him inside that world with her. She had talked about the first time she had fallen in love. With a book. An enchanted land filled with fairies, pixies, and exotic creatures. A place where people ate things like treacle and scones.

He had watched her as she spoke, drawn to the cadence of her voice, the natural planes of her face, the unblemished contours of her skin.

He had drunk it all in, the words themselves making little sense but a language far more primal filling the gap between them.

She had been bored one summer and read every text book cover to cover. She loved words. Loved how they came together to make beautiful things come alive. It is like painting, she had said, looking at him as if that would make more sense to him than what she had been saying about words and reading.

She had spoken of how she had taken to using the dictionary to play a game. Pointing to a word, reading its meaning, and picking another word from there and going on a hot chase to learn as many words as she could. She had turned a little pink, afraid she had shared too much as she talked about discovering the different words for sex and pleasure.

He had listened, struck by the ease she felt in talking about something reserved for the dark cover of the night. She had shone a spotlight on how limited his views were and how much, bigger the world was than he had known. In many ways, he had forgotten she was a woman; she was the closest to a friend, an equal partner, he could ever have had.

She had taken to devouring books because they transported her far, far away into countries where men treated women differently. Countries where women had dreams. They drove cars. They worked for a living. They were brave and strong and independent. With every book, her dreams of flying away had taken root. Someday, she would be on a plane to a faraway land, she had said. She would earn a lot of money. She would be an equal in a partnership. The boy who married her would respect her, she had said.

She had paused, gauging his reaction. Surya had been hooked. She reminded him of a bird, ready to soar, leaving them all behind.

The more Sandhya talked, the more he had imagined flying with her, soaring through the skies, and exploring faraway lands. But he had always landed with a thud, the pull of the roots and earth that bound him too strong for his wish to fly. He had tried imagining Sandhya in his home, on his land, in his family. The image had been hard to capture, even in his head. She was not meant for the land nor he for the skies.

He had taken to coming in early a few times a week. Almost always, watching her for a while before he announced his presence. They had gone from talking about books to discussing his work, his aspirations, and his view of the future. She had been fascinated by how his father ran the business. She had wanted to know how the credit system worked. "What do you do when people default?" she had asked. "No one defaults," he had replied and left it at that. But she had probed, wanting to watch a katta panchayat in action. The two of them had dragged Vennila to one of the villages along the Sirumugai-Gobichettipalayam route and stuck around the fringes, watching as the village council meted out justice quickly and brutally. Sandhya had averted her eyes from the sight of the punishment in action and fallen silent on their way back. Vennila had seemed unaffected, things like this as much part of her heritage as Surya was.

They had talked about women's rights. They had talked about growing up in a gender-biased world. The words had bubbled out of her as though the lid had been blown off her feelings. She had spoken of her growing up years. She had spoken of the kind of secrets that the girls in her school had talked about. The kinds of things that had made her view the men in her life with wariness. She feared most men, she had admitted.

"You have good reason to be scared, Sandhya, the men out there are not good people. Why do you think I never let you get on my bike or go alone with me anywhere? This is a small town. All it takes is a whisper of a rumor to demolish all the dreams you are building," Surya had said.

"Vennila, for all that she is the smartest in class, will never work. She may help her husband run his business, but that is about the most she will have the permission to do. It is not just me or her. It is the reality of the world we live in. You have dreams because you believe you can fly. Some of us do not have wings, Sandhya. We are like trees, rooted, bound to this earth," he had thought.

He had wanted to envelop her in a hug then, to reassure her that not all men were the same. He should have said then that all he wanted to do was to keep her safe in his little bubble, his and his only. The irony of this feeling had not been lost on him even then.

No one had really asked him questions the way she did, probing and desperately wanting to know. With each passing day, she had peeled a layer off him that he had never shared with anyone. She had once told him she wanted to know him inside out, like in the song by Bryan Adams. He had nodded, clueless, and then on his way home, gone to a cassette shop in town to find out what that song was about.

He had loved that about her, her ability to travel the world with her books. The way she analyzed song lyrics and listened to them with her eyes closed. He had noticed the shape of her eyebrows, the length of her

her eyelashes and the precise way her cheeks rounded out when she smiled. She was not beautiful in a classic way. She was not cool the way girls from Madras usually were, with their fitted tees and snug jeans. Instead, she had flitted in between, pairing jeans with an embroidered kurta, combing her hair without a part, tying it at the top of her head and braiding it after. There was something about her that riveted him, something indefinable. Being with her made him aspire for things he had deemed out of reach. She made him dream of a world beyond his view. She sat by the window, pointing to a speck in the horizon, knowing that one day she would be on board one of those. The certainty of her convictions had amazed him and drawn him to her.

As their final year had begun, he had felt a despondency descend, a sense of unease clawing at him. He had seen Aditya wait for Sandhya by the library. He had watched them sit side by side as they worked on their college applications. He had gone home to look up where Drexel, OSU and Villanova were. For the first time in his life, he had felt like a frog in a pond. The rootedness he had felt in his town, in his dad's business, had suddenly felt constraining. He had questioned the prevalent mindsets. He had looked at the women in his life with new eyes, wondering what held them back. For the first time in his life, he had wondered what it would be like to live his life with someone he respected. He had longed to fly, to soar with Sandhya.

Vennila had surprised them both one day, asking if they were in love. He had stuttered and blurted out that they were friends. Sandhya had remained silent and after his reply, copped to being just friends. Nothing more. Nothing less.

He had stalked off, disappearing from classes for the rest of the day. He had spent the day roaming the stadium trying to make sense of his feelings. What did it mean? That fuzzy line between friendship and love? Would he be ever able to leave behind what he considered his legacy to build a life afar? Would he be able to look his parents and Vennila's parents in the eye and tell them that he was betraying their trust? Would Sandhya fit into his life? Could he carve a Sandhya-shaped world in his life? Was it right for him to expect her to give up her dreams and stay tied to Coimbatore? Was it fair of her to expect him to give up his world and build a new world afar? As much as he loved her dreams, he could not see himself putting down roots anywhere else. It was not fair, this whole idea of love, the sacrificing of one self for another. He would be the practical man he always had been. She would fly. He would stay.

He had distanced himself from her, cooling the flames on their unsated desire. He had poured himself into business, channeling his angst into something productive. He had widened his horizons, looking at opportunities beyond their shores.

The last day of college he had spent with Vennila and Sandhya, her accidental touches and grazes burning marks on his skin. He had hummed with need, getting drunk on the time that was closing in on them. They had promised to keep in touch. They had walked along the gray lines of dusk, dipping their toes into uncharted waters. They had held hands, feeling a fuzz of warmth envelop them. Their reverie had been broken by the sound of Vennila running away from them.

Sandhya had wrenched her hand free as if breaking water for air. She had motioned for him to follow Vennila, muttering something about a book Aditya had given her that she had misplaced. As she disappeared into the tree-lined path where they had been sitting earlier and he had run toward the gate, she had said she would be back.

The reality of his situation had hit him as he watched Vennila muffling tears into her handkerchief. At that moment he had known his world would never be large enough for Sandhya and her dreams. He had to let her fly away.

———————

VENNILA AND SURYA: REFLECTIONS

Surya lets himself in, realizing he has been out longer than expected. He thinks of Vennila and their relationship. She had unquestioningly accepted him, molding her life around his dreams. She had been patient with him for much longer than he could remember, never once mentioning Sandhya. We were meant to be, she had told him once, meaning it with every fiber of her being. She had accepted his lapse with a grace he felt indebted to. A light glows in the living room as he steps in. Vennila is on the sofa, waiting for him.

The TV is off and the laptop lies on the sofa next to Vennila. He feels a surge of affection at the sight of her. He sits next to her and they hold hands, ruminating on their shared past. They had married right after college, Vennila's parents unwilling to wait for a few more years. Surya had agreed. They had fallen into the rhythms of domestic life without major adjustments. He had taken over his father's business and she had taken over the running of their joint family home. Shyam had arrived a year later and their lives had revolved around him.

"Are you okay? You took a long walk" Vennila asks, her voice soft, concerned.

Surya nods.

"I needed the time to think. What we saw on TV today brought it all back to me. Whenever they talk of the girl on TV, I think of Sandhya.

I wonder what happened to her after she left. I did not have the guts to find out. I have wondered enough though…"

Vennila turns to him. His shoulders are slumped; he looks broken.

"What really happened, Surya?"

Surya knows Vennila is not talking about the TV anymore.

"Do you really want to know, Nila? Some things are best left unsaid."

"I do, Surya. I deserve the truth. I know the two of you were in love. I also knew you would never leave this town. I loved you enough to accept a second place in your heart. I have never doubted your love for me, but it is not quite the same, is it?"

"Oh Nila, I love you. I do. What I feel for you is different but over the years, I have realized what we have together is lasting. I'm sorry you felt you were second best. I am honest when I say I have never thought of a life with Sandhya since the moment I married you. I have only been yours in thought and body. I want you to know that.

"I will tell you what happened but I want you to know the person I am today is not the person I was then."

Surya pauses, takes a deep breath and talks.

"After I dropped you both off at the hospital, I told my athai to prepare the report and send it to the college. I had also told the administrative officer that he will get a report and that he must do what he can to keep this under wraps."

He smiles wryly, wondering if he had really been that naive.

"Nila, I can't believe I actually believed her reputation was more important than punishing those guys." He looks at her, his eyes sorrowful.

"Surya, it was fourteen years ago. It was a different world then. Reputation did matter. Do you think she would have been able to get on with her life if she had filed a complaint? Do you remember our neighbor in Sirumugai? One whisper of scandal and she remained a spinster all her life. It was a big deal then. Probably is, even today."

Realizing Vennila had said what she had to say, Surya continued.

"I could not let Sandhya go unavenged. I had Aditya call Vetri and arrange for them to meet near Hope College Hotel. Aditya was reluctant but agreed after I promised he would not be involved in anything that happened. I made sure he was seen at the hostel mess by Vetri's friends."

Surya pauses to let what he is saying sink in. Vennila's face is impassive. She nods, urging him to continue.

"Later that evening, I had my gang, some from the med school, and, a few guys from the village wait near the hotel. We made Vetri and Rajesh get in the car and drove out to the farmhouse. We castrated them and I broke their fingers."

They sit in silence reliving the horror of the day.

Vennila realizes he is reliving that day in Coimbatore . Reaching for his hands, she holds them together and kneels in front of him. She lifts his chin, looks him in the eye and quietly forgives him. "Go on. I want to know it all," she adds softly.

"After what they did to Sandhya, I could not bear to imagine them going on to have a family life. We took videos of what we did to them and threatened to expose them if ever they thought of harming Aditya or anyone connected to the incident. From what I heard, they were left in front of their homes later that night. They left town and never returned."

Surya breaks down, sobbing. Vennila listens, adjusting herself next to him, holding his face tenderly in her hands as he lets go of the guilt he has been carrying around.

"Then?" she whispers.

"I did not want Sandhya to know what had been done to her, so I had Athai fudge Sandhya's records to show that they had gotten rough with her, but there hadn't been rape. I thought I had done what was best for her, for her reputation, but today I am weighed by the enormity of that decision."

Looking up at Vennila, he sees understanding and empathy in her eyes.

"When she repeatedly asked me what happened to her, I felt a blind rage course through me. How could I tell her Vennila? How could I?

If I had told her what I had done to Vetri and Rajesh, she would have seen me as an animal. I do not know if I could have lived with that."

He breaks down again.

"I wanted to protect her. Plus, with the guys involved, there was no telling what would have happened if she had pursued a case. Now I am no longer sure.

Who was I to decide anything for her, Vennila? I denied her a chance for justice. I denied her the grief she was allowed to feel. She wanted to know everything. Who were her rapists? What did they do to her? I could not tell her, Vennila. I could not.

Watching the coverage on TV brings it all back. The pain, the helplessness, the raw anger. I wish I could have held Sandhya instead and told her that she was not to blame. That they were the animals. That she would heal and the monsters who attacked her would receive their dues. But I did the only thing I could."

"Would they have received their dues, Surya?" Vennila asks. She is shaking her head. "I do not know about Sandhya, but if it had been me in her place, I would have been happy to know the animals who ravaged me were punished without hope for redemption. Think of me as you will, but I have no mercy for people who ruin others' lives because they are drunk on power."

Surya's hands are on his face and he is shaking uncontrollably. Vennila is crying too. They sit in silence, mourning all that was and all that could have been. The specter of rape that has haunted them for years is now playing out on live television.

———————

SANDHYA: TIS THE HOLIDAY SEASON

17 December, 2012

Malvern, PA

"Rashmi!" Sandhya exclaims as she picks up the phone. "Long time, no hear! How have you been?"

"I know! We are doing well. Sorry I have not called in such a long time. But then you have not either." Rashmi chuckles after an awkward pause and continues. "Well, the reason I am calling is that we are having a get-together at our home in Wayne this Saturday, 22 December. Mostly folks you know and a few who are new. Say you'll come please. Pretty please!" she pauses, waiting for Sandhya to say something.

Sandhya laughs as she replies, "Let me check my calendar, talk to Vikram and let you know."

"I will stay on the phone, please pull up your calendar and if Vikram is around, check with him. I do not have the time to send out an e-vite and then wait for folks to respond. I figured doing it over the phone will force people to let me know one way or another."

Sandhya puts the phone on mute while she calls out to Vikram.

"Vikram, Rashmi is on the phone. She wants to know if we can make it to a holiday get-together at their home this Saturday. What do you think?"

Vikram looks up from the iPad where he has been catching up on the news and scowls.

"Rashmi? Why is she calling now? We haven't been in touch for ages. Do you really want to go? It is up to you Sandhu. I'm okay if you want to go though of course I'd rather stay home and catch the game on TV. But will you be okay among the babies and mom talk? You know it upsets you."

Sandhya thinks for a moment and un-mutes the phone.

"Okay! We are free that Saturday. Count us in. If Vikram has an emergency to attend to that day, he can join us when he is done. Sound okay?"

"Done! See you then. I have a few more calls to make. Toodleloo!" Rashmi hangs up.

Sandhya puts the phone back into its cradle and wonders why she agreed. Rashmi and she go back almost ten years. They had been acquaintances turned good friends. Infertility had bound them tighter. They had the same doctors, discussed protocols, cheered each other on and grieved with one other when their cycles failed. All that had changed one cycle when Sandhya had miscarried while Rashmi had gone on to have Vibha.

There had been no falling out. Rashmi had walked on eggshells around Sandhya. Sandhya had resented what fate had dealt her. They had let too much time pass between phone calls. Then one summer before Vibha turned five, Rashmi had moved to a nearby town with a better school district and a home with a yard. With her had gone the little reason they had had to run into each other. Rashmi had continued to send the annual holiday cards. The first couple of times, Sandhya had replied over email. After that she had put them away with the trash.

"Do you really want to go?" Vikram's voice intrudes into her thoughts. She looks up. "Why not? It's been a long time. I am not even sure why we stopped talking. Maybe this will be a chance to meet other folks too.

"I have grieved enough, Vikku. What is wrong with us cannot be solved by pushing people away. I am tired of being sad and angry all the time. Honestly, I think I will learn to embrace the term childfree."

Vikram gives in and nods. Sandhya pushes a plate of toast and omelet towards him. They eat in silence at the kitchen island. Vikram is dressed for a cold day in the field. Faded corduroys. Plaid, fleece-lined hooded shirt and thick socks. Sandhya watches him finish his plate, wash up and put on his rugged boots. He remembers his gloves and jacket before he heads out. "You have a fun day!" calls Sandhya as he leaves in his old but trusty pickup.

Vikram works with a veterinary practice servicing the farms around their town. His occupation is unusual in their circles. It is perhaps why she had been drawn to him. She mulls it over in her head as she makes her way upstairs to shower and get ready for work.

Sandhya works for a bank. She had started out as an intern on her work permit, slowly working her way up to being a business analyst. She has a busy couple of days coming up before a two-day conference at the head office in Philadelphia starting Thursday. She is working on a product demo for the management team from the company acquiring them. She sighs at the thought of taking the train to the city.

An hour later, she is logged in and getting started on her emails when her phone buzzes with a message from her mother. "Amma! Why are you texting me? If you want me to call, just say so!" she teases her mom over text.

Without waiting for her mom to reply, she picks up the phone and calls India to catch up quickly.

"Eppadi irrukae? I just felt like talking to you. You did not call in the morning like you usually do."

Something about her mom's tone gives Sandhya pause.

"Are you okay, Amma? You sound strange. Is Appa okay? I want to talk to him. I was on the phone with Rashmi, that is why I did not call."

"We are all fine, kannu." She pauses and then continues. "Have you seen the news from India this morning?"

Puzzled, Sandhya answers in the negative and pulls up Google News on her phone. Switching it to region India, the very first headline hits her like a punch to the gut.

"*Gang rape!*" "*Rape victim critical!*" "*Nirbhaya!*" "*Protests!*" Her eyes skim, flitting from keyword to keyword as she begins to understand why her mother is upset.

"I have not, Amma. Should I?"

"No, avoid the news if you can. It is graphic and it will upset you." The concern in her mom's voice sets off a series of alarms in her head.

"I will be okay, Amma. I have been okay for years now. Please don't worry. I have to work. Tell Appa I will talk to him your time in the morning. Don't worry, Amma. I love you."

Sandhya hangs up and clicks through the first headline. The next thing she knows it is almost noon and she has done little but devour every piece of news on the rape. She realizes that reading through it like is cutting open old wounds and ripping the Band-Aid off healing cuts. Yet, she is unable to stop. Perhaps part of her hunger to learn everything about the case is fueled by how little she knows of what happened to her. She knows she had been assaulted. But that is all she knows.

An incoming call drags her out of the news reports and back to work. Emails pile up with FAQs on the merger and the work streams that are being reorganized. She leaves them unread, knowing there is little she can do to change the outcomes if any. The rest of the day flies past and the sound of the garage opening lets her know that Vikram is back. She logs off and sets a pot of water for the tea. It is just Monday and she is already longing for the weekend.

"How was your day?"

Vikram grunts as he pulls his boots off and throws his shirt in the laundry. "I'll have a shower and then fill you in." She watches as he disappears up the stairs. The sight of him fills her with warmth. Solid, steady, dependable. They have been married twelve years now. The sounds of the shower running reminds her to check the stove and she brews two cups of strong tea with ginger. Vikram joins her as she sets the tea and a plate of mini samosas warm from oven on the kitchen island.

"I had a good day. Had to stop by Organic Acres to look at some of their livestock. Then I made it to the Moo-fresh creamery. Sally delivered today." He winks at her as he continues. "I put a pint of freshly-made mint chocolate chip ice-cream in the freezer."

He seems happy and rambles on about his various patients. Sandhya listens, happy to listen to the sound of his voice as it rises and falls. She takes in his relaxed demeanor and obvious joy in what he does for a living and it makes her happy.

He asks, "How was yours?" Sandhya wonders if she should mention the news Amma had talked to her about. She demurs, thinking it best not to let it intrude into their evening. "Morning was awash with emails to catch up on. The afternoon was better. Got some work done. Of course, with the holiday season, more than half the team is on vacation. Every year I think I should take the last two weeks off but it never happens, does it? I love this time of the year."

She sighs. Vikram suggests they go for a walk after dinner to look at the holiday lights around their neighborhood.

They live in a valley, a fact that is brought home each time they drive home from anywhere. The view of the lights twinkling at them as they course through the highway screams a welcome. The hillocks that frame the development they live in has tiny trails and beautiful views. The nearest grocery store is four miles away. The street names are quaint and a throwback to quieter, less populated times. They have put down roots that grow thicker with each passing year and emphasize the hyphen in their Indian-American identity.

They walk, bundled up for the weather, and stop at each display. Sandhya reaches for his gloved arm and links hers in it. As they reach the end of the cul-de-sac, she brings up what her mom had called about. Vikram listens without interrupting. When she is done, he pauses, looks her in the eye and draws her in for a hug. What he cannot seem to say in words, he pours it into the hug, hoping his love will be enough to slay the demons. Sandhya stays in his arms, accepting his warmth and wishing for a day when she can erase the past from her head. He holds her close and they make their way back home.

———————

VIKRAM: LINGERING SHADOWS

Settling into bed, Vikram props himself against his pillow, urging Sandhya to lean against him. He combs through her hair with his fingers, making slow, hypnotizing patterns. He watches her sink into sleep, her body snuggled against his.

His mind is far away in Madras. He had grown up hearing his mother whimper as he slept. His father, an academician at the local university, had been well respected. He had exuded an air of authority. He had been the first to show up at funerals and the last to leave at weddings. He had loved commanding and organizing anything to do with the small block of flats they had lived in.

Inside the home though, he had ruled with an iron hand. As an only child, Vikram had been spared the worst of it. While he had never seen his dad lay a hand on his Amma, her sobs at night and the strange bruises on her arms and sometimes neck told a different story. He had grown increasingly alarmed and doubled his efforts to do things for his mom in his silent way. His eyes had spoken where words could have made no sense.

He had questioned his dad once, in a rare moment of courage. The venom in his dad's eyes had chilled him. His mom had borne the bruises of that conversation for a week after. He had resolved to study hard, get his mom and himself out of that evil man's grasp as soon as he could.

The fire that had been lit in his belly that week became an inexhaustible flame that made him view the world very differently than his friends did.

When his dad had died a little over a year after Vikram had left home, he had sighed in relief. His mom remained stoic, saying nothing, never bad-mouthing the man who had been his father.

As an adult he had often asked his mom why she had never left. Her answer always had been, "Where would we have gone? My family members had their own problems, why would they have taken responsibility for me and you? I never was permitted to work even if I wanted to. I had no money. I told myself that one day you would be an adult and I would finally leave him and go someplace where I could help women like me.

"Vikku, promise me that you will never be blind to the problems of the women in your life. There is no point celebrating or mourning a person's life after they are gone. The joy is in the here and now. When you marry, I want you and your wife to be happy. Never look past the hurt in her eyes. Also, I will never come and live with you. I will watch from afar and be happy that your life is nothing like mine. When I die, Vikku, I don't want you to mourn me or do any of the rituals your Appa forced me to participate in for his forefathers. I hate religion. I hate the pretense of caring for people after they are gone.

"Will you remember? Honor me when I am alive. Treat the women in your life with respect. Never look away if someone is being abused..."

She had broken down, overcome with emotion. Vikram had held

her and promised himself that he would always look out for the people in his life. He had not given marriage or women much thought. His life had been taken over by proving himself to be better than his father. He had bucked convention and chosen animal husbandry over dental college. His father had been livid but Vikram had quietly gone about what he had needed to do. That he had managed a stipend and a scholarship was something his father could not ignore. He had grudgingly come around and by the time Vikram had left for America for higher studies, his father had even sung praises of his son.

After his father's death, his mom, true to her word, had become a champion for the people around her who were abused. He would often call home to find his mom tending to or championing the cause of a woman she knew needed help. He worried about her tendency to let strangers in her home but also knew enough to not be his father and take away her agency. He did what he could, calling to check on her every day and supporting her financially in a way that made it feel less like support and more like autonomy.

———————

SANDHYA: THE STUFF OF NIGHTMARES

Vikram watches a game on TV while Sandhya catches up on work before bed. They head upstairs together. As if anticipating a choppy night, Vikram holds her close and combs through her hair with his fingers as she falls asleep to the reassuring murmur of his heartbeat.

She slips in and out of dreams.

She is sitting in the classroom, her feet propped up on the chair next to her. She is lost in Pride and Prejudice, laughing at Mr. Collins's pomposity, when a sound startles her. Surya is framed against the entrance of the classroom, looking taller and scrawnier than he usually does. Her heart does a slow flip. He is not handsome by any standard, but there is an intensity about him that captivates her.

She is sitting by the trees, laughing at something Vennila said when Surya roars in on his bike, his black helmet and windbreaker giving him the aura of a cinema hero. She watches him dismount and hastily looks away when he comes closer. He drops down next to Vennila and reaches for her lunch box. She watches as he devours Vennila's food like it is his birthright.

She is standing at the bus stop, her dupatta flapping in the wind. It covers his face and for a moment, it is just him and her in a purple haze.

He brings it to her and wraps it around her, a moment so intimate that she feels it in the pit of her stomach.

They are in a dark movie hall watching a Kamal Hassan starrer. She has a bag of popcorn open, dipping into it at regular intervals when she finds his hand instead. They linger, neither moving, lost in the moment and oblivious of what is playing on the screen.

It is her birthday, she is wearing the red and black salwar Amma had sent her, her hair is loose. She sticks a bindi on her face and for a moment imagines herself a bride, resplendent in red, Surya reflected in the mirror in front of her.

She is in the canteen, Aditya across from her. She slides a bookmark out. The one she had gotten at Greetings Galore, the greeting card and gift shop near college. She had gone all the way into town, to Gandhipuram, to have it etched with his initials. She is not sure why she did it. But the pleasure on his face as he turns it over makes her feel warm all over. She realizes she has known Aditya for a long time now. Perhaps, it is the fact that they will be flying to unknown lands together, but she feels connected to him.

She is wearing a yellow kurta, the color of sunflowers. She is happy, she is singing. She is flapping her hands; she is a bird. They all laugh. Gorgeous, unaffected laughs. Vennila touches her lightly on her arm. She is not vocal, but she feels deeply. The immensity of it being the last day of college is weighing her down.

The mood changes, the sun is hidden behind the clouds. Vennila asks her gently. "You will keep in touch, won't you? You won't forget these villager friends, right?" She laughs, her happiness tempered by *sadness. It is bittersweet.*

"And you and Surya will get married right?" Sandhya asks. Her voice a little too bright. A hush falls on their little group. They walk, their feet carrying them of their own accord to their own little place in between two trees, their wide branches meeting and forming a canopy. The sunlight filters through. The dirt floor dances with the light, as if part of a magic kingdom. They put their bags down, lean against the brick wall, their knees pulled up to their chins. The mood is somber.

The sun breaks through, flooding them with light. Vennila and Surya are sitting with her. She has a journal in her hands and she is passing it to Surya. He looks at it and returns it untouched.

"Why?" she asks.

"I have nothing to say," he says dryly and looks at Vennila instead. Vennila pulls it from her and in her loopy, cursive script writes: "Reach for the skies, Sandhya. You are meant to fly. Someday, when you look down, I will be waving at you. Ever your friend, Vennila."

Sandhya closes the journal and puts it into her backpack. She pulls out the book Aditya had given her earlier. She holds it out for Vennila to inspect.

"Roots by Alex Haley." Vennila reads the back cover and seems interested. She asks, "Why did he give you this book?"

"He thinks I should understand how America was built. Out of the blood and sweat of people like us," Sandhya smirks. "I've just started to read it. I hope to finish it before I leave." She holds the book in her hands and turns to look at Surya. He has a faraway expression on his face. Nudging him, she asks what he is thinking about. He pauses before he answers,

"Can you really make a home in the clouds?"

He seems childlike now, trying to grasp whatever is left of the fleeting time they have together. She feels an enormous urge to trace her finger along his face. Feel the stubble on his cheek. Feel his lips on hers. As if ashamed by her thoughts, she rises. The emotions that have been simmering at the pit of her stomach threaten to overwhelm her. "Let's get a cup of kaapi at the petty kadai before I head back to the hostel. Our last cuppa before who knows when we will meet again." She strides along the dirt path with the easy grace of one who knows what she wants.

They walk along, Vennila overtaking them. Their hands brush and Surya's hand finds hers. She can feel the blood pulsing under his skin. She feels alive. Wanted. For a moment she wonders what it will be like to let go of her dreams to fly away. To put down roots instead. To stay with Surya as he builds his business empire. Perhaps the intensity of her thoughts touch Vennila. She turns back and the shock she registers at their linked hands and the bubble that envelops them brings Sandhya out of her reverie. Vennila runs and Surya runs behind her.

Sandhya hefts her backpack and realizes she left the book behind. She calls out to Surya, telling him she will be back. She walks back, lost in thought. What does she really want? She has known for a long time that Vennila is in love with Surya. Her relationship with Surya is one that has no name. They had muddled along, hiding their chemistry behind the facade of friendship. They had shared intimate details of their lives, talking about the future, each careful to exclude the other from it.

Then, there's Aditya. He had shown signs over the past year of being interested in her. They share a common love of books and a desire to fly to faraway lands. Yet, something about Surya pulls her to him. She feels drawn to him like a moth to a light. She pauses at the thought of the word that has entered her consciousness. Is she in love? Is this how it feels?

Her thoughts are interrupted by jeers and catcalls. "Boys!" she thinks, and shakes her head. She needs to hurry up, get the book and clear out of there. There had always been rumors about shady stuff happening at the stadium after dark.

"Adhopaaru da, Aditya aalu! (Look who's here, Aditya's girl!)"

"Mel padippupadikka America pogudhaam. (She is flying to the US for higher studies)"

She looks up to see Rajesh, a boy from Aditya's class, looking at her hungrily. She had always disliked him. His eyes are looking at her breasts, fascinated. She feels around her neck for a dupatta, realizing this is a kurta that did not have one. A thread of fear snakes from her back to her neck. She considers making a run for it. Instead, she pretends to be cool and continues walking towards the tree where she had left the book behind. Spying it, she feels relief. As she rushes to pick it up and run, the voices sound close. Too close. She can smell the booze before she can see them. A cloying smell of alcohol and sweat.

The taunts continue, Vetri joining in.

"Semma figure illa? Aaana enna maami maari dress pannara illa? Kelati paakalama? (Nice ass. She dresses like an auntie, should we take her clothes off to look?)"

The fear that had been fleeting is now a solid wall. She steps back, grabs the book, adjusts her bag, and makes a run for it when Rajesh puts his leg out and trips her. She falls, a fall that seems endless. The trees swim before her eyes, she flails, clawing the air on her way to the ground. The book flies, the bag falls with a thud before she does.

She remembers the crack, the sound of a coconut breaking, as her head connects with the rock. She remembers stars, laughter and little else. Everything seems amplified. The world around her weaves and spins. She remembers pain. Shooting, blinding pain. She feels their weight on her. She can feel fingers pawing her. Rough palms grabbing at what they can find. She feels like a carcass with scavengers making off whatever they can.

She screams, trying to get up. She finds she has lost her voice. She tries to open her eyes and all she can see are shadowy images. She feels wetness, plundering mouths and a weight she can no longer bear. She gasps for air, weakly moves her arms as if batting away the invisible arms and faces. She can feel the chill as her bare skin is exposed, the salty taste of blood in her mouth as she bites herself. She can smell crushed grass, something trickling down her cheek and the rusty smell of blood. Her voice comes back. She screams, a guttural cry that rises from the pit of her stomach and resounds in her brain, amplified against the night sky.

Suddenly the weight is off her and she is floating. She feels like a feather, disembodied. She wants to sink into a deep, bottomless sleep.

———

"Saṇdhya, Sandhya…" The voice is familiar.

"Aditya?" She murmurs. She opens her eyes to find Vikram holding and rocking her. Her nightshirt is damp with sweat. A sheen of moisture lines her face. Her heart is racing. The lights are on. She is safe. She is home. Tears engulf her. She is not sure if she is crying for the Sandhya she was or the Sandhya she is.

VIKRAM: SOMETIMES HOME IS A PERSON

Vikram rubs Sandhya's back, wishing he could pour himself into her, assuage her fears, wipe away those tears and vanquish the demons that haunt her. He looks at the woman in front of him. Tears have streaked a path along her cheeks, flowing into her dark blue sleep shirt. Her body is convulsed with emotion. She is rocking back and forth, leaning against him for comfort. He hurts for her. He hurts with her. At times like this, he wishes he could find the men who ravaged her and tear them from limb to limb. He cannot comprehend what could possibly cause a bunch of men to act this way.

Vikram is taken back twelve years. To the first time he was witness to Sandhya's nightmares. He had been warned. Sandhya had told him in no uncertain terms that she was broken. A part of her was a huge void for which she had no matching pieces. He had wanted to make her whole. To fill that void with all the love he could pour into it.

Sandhya had come into his life like a sunbeam. Hers had been one of the many turmeric-edged jadagams that had found their way to his home, a modest two-storied building in one of the quieter residential areas of Madras. (He could never bring himself to call his hometown Chennai.) He had been on vacation, visiting his mom for a month. "Do you have a girlfriend?" his mom had asked, a prayer patent on her face that his answer would be "No." He had smiled and replied, "No." Her pleasure at being able to play matchmaker for him overrode any objections he had had to being part of an arranged marriage. He had leafed through the natal charts curiously, amused at how similar they all were.

"Fair," "Beautiful," "Slim," "Enjoys cooking," "Homely..." The descriptions of the women had reminded him of his patients, the many docile cows he tended to everyday. They were calm, happy to be handled and their liquid brown eyes were the picture of a deep, placid serenity. The pictures accompanying the charts were eerily similar too, all the women posing stiffly at a studio, with excessive powder on the face, a forced smile and neatly groomed hair. He had not been sure what he had been looking for, but it had not been this. He had wanted to see someone who called out to him.

When his eyes had met Sandhya's in the photograph attached to her chart, he had known. The photographer had clearly taken her unawares. She had been wearing a bright blue salwar and her hair had been tucked behind her ears, lying in waves around her shoulders. She had been leaning against a pillar, probably lost in thought when someone familiar had called out to her. Her face had that element of surprise, pleasure at seeing someone close to her; her smile was genuine, reaching all the way to her eyes.

He had wanted to ask her about the picture. About the photographer who had evoked such joy in her. Her bio had been short. Five feet six inches, wheat complexioned, slim. Working for a banking services company in Bangalore. Her interests had been listed as reading and cooking. He had read the bio a couple of times. It had to have been written by her parents.

"This one," he had told his mother and she had dutifully reached out to Sandhya's parents. It turned out that Sandhya's mother Savithri had been his mother's classmate at school. Sandhya's father, Jayaraman, worked in the Defense Accounts office with his aunt Chitra. Theirs was a modest middle-class family. Sandhya's sister Usha was married and settled in California. They had only one request. Sandhya wanted the prospective suitor to make the trip to Bangalore and meet her in person, alone.

Intrigued by Sandhya's stance and her parents' curious acceptance of it, he had agreed. His mom had been thrilled.

"Go, talk to her. Get to know her. Be respectful and give her the space she needs. I will love anyone who you like."

Vikram thought of all the ways his mom could have turned the tables, grabbing power to subvert what had been done to her. Yet, all she had thought of was his happiness and that of the woman he would choose to be part of their family. He was proud of being her son.

He had boarded the train from Madras to Bangalore in the morning, enjoying his time away from the predictable routine he had settled into. The towns and villages had sped past, punctuated by stops where vendors hawked tea, coffee, and snacks. He had purchased a bottle of water, tea, and a plate of bajjis knowing his mother wouldn't have approved.

The journey had taken him back in time to his summer vacations to Mettupalayam. They had traveled as a family, packing food and snacks for the 10-hour trip from door to door. He had cherished those vacations and the bonds he had formed with the children near his thatha's house. Visiting only for the summer, he had been their source for all things Madras. Beaches. Oh! The beaches. He had never understood their fascination with Marina beach. He had had to describe it all to them, making sure to include the stray dogs, the smell of wet fishing nets and the crap he had to watch out for in order to avoid stepping in it. His eyes had twinkled even as he had retched, pretending the smell was so gross, he couldn't handle it.

They had roamed the streets, feeding stray dogs and cows, hopping over fences to explore the betel orchards. He had discovered his love for animals in that small town that had smelled of cabbages. He had seen older men handle their livestock gently, perform sterilizations with a compassion that belied what was being done. He had watched, fascinated.

At one time he had witnessed their katta panchayat, the dispensation of justice by the village council that had seemed barbaric but timely. It had made him wonder if vigilante justice perhaps had its place in society. But then he had shaken his head refusing to get drawn into the murky thoughts he had been keeping at bay for a few years. . There had been days when he had had vivid images of butchering his father, watching as he writhed in pain, powerless against his son. He had woken up from dreams worried he had the makings of a murderer in himself. He had worried that his shadow side would be revealed for all to see and that his life as he knew it would end.

In Bangalore, he had parked his suitcase at his cousin Raghu's bachelor pad and gotten ready to meet Sandhya for an early dinner at a restaurant in Indira Nagar.

The modest entrance of the restaurant had opened into a large place inside. He had picked a table from where he could see when she arrived. She had shown up in jeans and a tee, hair tied neatly in a ponytail. She had stood at the entrance, her profile athletic and sharp, scanning the crowd before settling on him. Her stride had been long and her demeanor confident.

Her handshake had been firm, warm, and friendly. She had held his eyes through dinner as they exchanged notes on where they had been to school, college and for graduate studies. She had talked about her work and insisted on paying for the meal, despite his protests.

"My town, my rules," she had quipped.

They had stepped out into the warm night and she had suggested taking an auto to somewhere near her home and walking the rest of the distance. Seated in an auto, her voice had been grave when she had turned to him and spoken.

"Have you really thought about marriage? What you want from it? How does a partner fit in your future?"

He had been struck by the way she had framed her questions and her choice of the word 'partner' instead of 'wife.' He had considered it and replied with gravity.

"I do not really know. I have not thought about it much. The idea of marriage is a vague concept. My mom was not happy in her marriage so all I know is that I do not want the woman in my life to ever feel like my mother did. Beyond that, not much…"

He had paused and then continued.

"Since you asked, this is what I think. I like you. You work just as I do. I like my life in the US. If you are open to relocating to the US, that will be great. If not, I can explore options here in Bangalore. I do not believe in long distance relationships. They may be okay for a while but the point of getting married is to stay together."

He had looked up and recognized approval in her eyes.

"Interesting. "Most men I have met have either assumed I would move or that I would find a way to fit my life into theirs. I like how you did not assume I would quit my job or want to relocate.

"Vikram, I am clear about certain things in my life. One, I am looking for a partner. That means someone who will walk with me, not lead, or follow. I also am looking for someone who will treat me with respect. Honesty is a big deal for me. There are things in my past I will want to talk about eventually. I have been through a lot and honestly, most people haven't gotten to the point where I have opened up to them."

The auto had stopped, but they had continued to talk late into the night, walking around the gated complex where she had lived with a roommate. When they were done, she had been spent and he was in love.

She had talked about college, about her love for her friend Surya. How she had admired his work ethic and burning desire to build something for himself. She had wanted that kind of ambition for herself and for the first time, she had realized she had to break free of the shackles she had imposed on herself. She had been animated when she had asked, "Why do I have to know to the ideals and rules that society imposes on me because of my gender?"

Vikram had fallen for her sparkling eyes and her spirited personality.

The last thing she had talked about was the assault. She had broken down as she had relived the pain and the isolation she had felt from the moment she had regained consciousness, spoken about her burning need for justice that had been suppressed by the need to keep her name pristine. Reputation. How she had hated that word! She had talked about how she had moved away from home, deferring her admission at Villanova and finally never getting her Master's degree. She had talked about her battles with depression, her attempts at therapy that had never given her the closure she craved. Eventually, she had turned work into therapy, pouring her energies and time into things she could control. Men at work had been interested in her, but she had never felt anyone could understand what she had been through and what that would mean for the rest of their lives.

She liked working in the finance domain, she had said. She had seemed knowledgeable about visa rules and how hard it was to find a job as a new immigrant. Eventually she had paused, stopping under the light of a lamppost, looked at him and said, "Vikram, I like that you look me in the eye. I like that you can listen. I like that you are respectful and honest. I am willing to explore this further but…" She had smiled and continued "…what do you like about me? Why do you want to marry me? You could have your pick of any number of women who come without baggage."

"I like you, Sandhya. I like you, baggage and all. Very rarely do I come across women who know what they want and are clear about it," he had said.

Just as he'd turned to leave, she had reached for his arm. A puzzled look on her face, she had asked, "Why animals? Why such a different line of work? Why the US?"

He had gone to her apartment with her, surprised by how spartan it was. Legs folded beneath him; he had made himself comfortable. Sandhya had brewed cups of tea and they had sat in the mellow light of a side table lamp as he told her all about himself.

"It starts with my name," he had said, laughing. "Vikram Vaidhyanathan." He had spoken of his annual trips to his maternal hometown, Mettupalayam near Coimbatore. The kids there had called him Vaidhyar, meaning doctor, because of his last name. It had stuck and perhaps because of that, when he had discovered a love for animals after he'd watched the birth of a calf, wide-eyed with horror and fascination, he had decided to be a vet.

His dad had wanted him to become a dentist because he knew people who could get him admission to Savitha Dental College. But a timely scholarship had convinced his dad to accept his decision to turn to animal husbandry. Then, the idea of spiting his dad had spurred him to do well.

Vikram had not lingered much on his dad, but made it clear that he hated the man and was happy he was dead. His eyes lit up when he spoke of his mom. She is all the family I have and need, he had said.

Following a PhD fellowship, he had moved to the US where he had become involved with organic farming and raising livestock.

He had no friends; he had stated baldly. Seeing Sandhya's raised eyebrows, he had clarified that he had a great many acquaintances, but was not particularly big on confidences or friendships that lasted over time.

"No girlfriends?" Her voice had been teasing. She had seemed surprised that he had none.

Reaching a lull in the conversation, he looked at the time and they had parted with promises to meet again over the next week. He had held her hand, lingering over it longer than necessary.

When the cab he had called arrived, Sandhya had stood by her window, watching him get into the car. On his way to Raghu's apartment, Vikram had been filled with thoughts about Sandhya's horrific rape, struggling with an overwhelming need for justice that had surprised him. "I'd castrate them if I could get a hold of them," had been his last thought as he turned in for the night, given the considerable experience he had with gelding.

The next couple of weeks had been a whirlwind. They had gone on a few more dates. Watched movies, sat in the park, held hands, and whispered sweet nothings. Their parents had arranged a formal engagement and one evening in July, they had exchanged garlands and committed to a wedding in October.

The wedding had been a grand event spread over three days with more than a thousand guests. Sandhya had been a beautiful bride. Her sister and family had flown in from California and Vikram had made friends with them easily.

Their first night together had been easy. They had simply passed out in exhaustion after Sandhya had meticulously washed off her makeup, untangled her tightly-braided hair and changed out of her heavy silks. Sandhya had been strangely unselfconscious. They had sat next to each other on their bridal bed, holding hands, agreeing to take their time, to date each other before attempting intimacy.

Their first few months of married life had flown in a haze of uprooting Sandhya from Bangalore and planting her in suburban Philadelphia. She had taken well to Malvern, with its winding roads and quaint charm. Her nightmares had come out of the blue, hitting Vikram with the enormity of what she had gone through. He had held her, promising not to force anything on her. She started to see a therapist to help her with her anxieties surrounding intimacy.

By the time their first anniversary had rolled around, Sandhya had declared she was ready. But Vikram had been scared. They had reached out to each other tentatively, uncertain of what would happen. They had ended up frustrated because Sandhya could not get past a barrier that seemed to have rooted somewhere deep inside her. Vikram had tried to hide his disappointment and it had made things worse.

Over the years, she had resisted less and less, allowing Vikram to enter her, but there was no joy in their union. He hated himself for what felt like a forced consummation. She said she wanted it for him, even if it gave her no joy herself. Their sex life was an uneasy truce made worse by a ticking biological clock.

Despite Sandhya's aversion to physical sex, she yearned to be a mother. She had hesitantly brought up the idea of going to a doctor to see why they had not become pregnant yet and Vikram had agreed. Privately, he thought she would be pregnant if it were not for the stress she carried within herself.

Over the years, the nightmares had lessened, occurring infrequently, often brought on only by triggers such as random newspaper articles, feminist rants, news on TV, tasteless jokes. Each time, Vikram had sat with her, soothing away her fears and tears.

Tonight's nightmare has been a break in the pattern. For the first time, she had called out a name. Aditya. That unsettled Vikram.

———————

UMA: MUSINGS ON ABUSE

17 December, 2012

Austin, US

Uma sorts through the laundry as she hums along with the radio playing on her phone, amplified by the Bluetooth speakers in the adjoining room. The whites and the colors sit in stacks as she starts on the ones that need additional TLC before they go into the wash. She picks up a crisp white shirt, holding it up to light as she inspects the collar and under arms for stains and stubborn patches. Nothing that a good scrub cannot handle, she decides. She holds his shirt under warm water from the faucet, adding soap and scrubbing until the bubbles wash off. Putting it to the side, she picks up a pair of her leggings. A rusty stain marks the back. Cursing, she scrubs hard, wondering why some stains do not come off.

Perhaps it is the sight of the stain or the strain of wanting a child, but tears threaten her. Suddenly, the music seems loud and jarring. She washes her hands and turns the radio off. She will get to the clothes that need a good scrub later. She loads the sorted whites, starts the load and, steps into the kitchen.

The counters gleam and there is a hint of mint in the air. The sink is empty, the dishwasher humming. She had packed pulao for Aditya and left the rest in a warm casserole. Now she does not even have to make lunch. She toys with the idea of a grocery run. The fridge is near empty and they are going away for the rest of the week. A restlessness has taken hold of her and she paces the room, looking for anything to work her frustration away.

There really is nothing for her to do, at least until the laundry needs folding. She walks towards her study and powers the laptop on. The clock shows 11:30 am. It is 10:00 pm India time, her mind calculates instantly. Her mom must be done for the day. For a moment she feels lonely and aches for her mom. For home.

The laptop boots and takes her to the browser that is loading Google News, her homepage. Her eyes skim the headlines. Politics does not interest her. Entertainment does. As she hovers over the tab, one of the headlines makes her sit up.

She spends the next hour reading about the protests and candlelight vigils for Nirbhaya. She wonders what about this case has grabbed her nation's fleeting attention. It isn't as if rapes are uncommon, she muses. Delhi is famous for it. She shakes her head as if unable to quite get what about it is bothering her.

She pulls up her Wordpress account. TheSunGoddess has been on quite a break, she mutters, smiling. She had started the blog on a whim while working for a startup that helped other companies figure out what to do with all the data on who was visiting their websites, who was clicking on what. She had loved it, looking for patterns, predicting what content would generate the most hits. Social media and digital trends were her thing. The blog was her way of playing around to see what worked and what did not.

She had also loved her workplace because the work life had been her social life. She had hung out with the same folks she worked with. Watching the women around her flirt, fall in love and get their hearts broken, she had figured she could comment on it columnist-style, a la Carrie of Sex and the City. Only she had gone on to chronicle her teenage infatuation with Aditya, whom she called Mister on the blog. Her posts had become popular and she had ridden the wave until she met Biker Dude and later, broke up with him. She had quit blogging for a while then, scared by the intensity of the comments on her post. While she had believed she was totally anonymous, she had also been afraid she would be outed.

She had started blogging again after she had moved to Austin, writing about her life there. She remembered fondly her only post with a picture. The one she had posted after she had gotten inked with a butterfly on her left shoulder. La Mariposa, she had titled the post. On an impulse she pulled it up.

• • • • • • • • • • • •

La Mariposa

Hola Amigos!

Guess what I did today? No peeking!

I got myself inked. A pretty little butterfly. Purple and green with a black edging. I think it is pretty even if I say so myself. Wanna see? Don't be shy!

So, that's one thing off my bucket list. Why a butterfly you ask?

I have always loved butterflies. They are pockets of sunshine that flit into and out of your life. The eggs hatch, become hairy caterpillars, metamorphose, and become beautiful butterflies. In some ways, I feel my life has gone through a lot of changes. I have hibernated and I am finally heading towards a life I have dreamed of for ages.

Voila! A butterfly to mark the milestone.

Love it? Hate it? Leave me a note.

Song recommendation: My Love - Justin Timberlake

• • • • • • • • • • • •

Perhaps all the world loved love stories and blogging from Austin, she had seemed to be drawing more readers than ever. But rereading her older posts one evening, she had realized she came across as a broken record. Since then, she has been on a mission to sway her content to general topics.

It occurs to her that she could make a post of her unease with the news today. If only she could figure out what about the Nirbhaya case was so haunting. Putting her laptop away, she walks to her closet and pulls out her sneakers. Half an hour on the treadmill will give her time to think.

She selects an auto curated playlist from her Saavn app and plugs her earphones in. "Thum Tak" from Raanjhanaa plays and she walks, getting lost in the music and the lyrics. That's when it hits her. The images from the song of the hero stalking the heroine paint a picture of what she had found hard to vocalize.

She forces herself to walk the thirty minutes she has set herself before she heads back to her trusty laptop. The words are swimming in her head, waiting for release.

• • • • • • • • • • • •

It could have been me

As news swirls of the Nirbhaya rape and the media and the public have taken to impassioned pleas for justice, I sit here in my modest suburban home wondering, why now? I look back on my growing years and remember the countless times I was flashed. I remember having my buttocks slapped, pinched and my breasts fondled as I stood sandwiched between strangers in a crowded bus. I coped by carrying safety pins, protecting my chest with solid files, and stamping on the feet of those who groped me. My friends and I shared tips on how to keep ourselves safe. We learned to walk home in groups and stay inside past the 8:00 pm mark.

Not once did we question why. We did it because, you know, boys will be boys and if we girls did not invite it, why would they resort to such behavior? I worried about my bra straps showing. I worried about clothing that *gasp* might outline my curves and invite lustful views and who knows what else. There are people in my circle who have had acid poured on their faces because they spurned uninvited advances. I have seen my friends not go on school trips because their parents were worried about what might happen on the one night their child was away from their watchful eyes.

Today, as I read of Nirbhaya and her friend, I realize why it affects me so much. It could have been me.

It could have been me.

I have stayed out later than 8:00 pm, walking home from a dinner out with friends. I have been out going on bike rides with my boyfriend. I have been out celebrating birthday parties in pubs. I have been out there, going about my life, getting in share autos and private cabs, naively believing that nothing would happen because I was dressed okay, because I had a friend with me.

It could have been me.

The men who raped and sodomized Nirbhaya did it because they were out to have a good time. They did it because she resisted. They did it because they were sick, demented animals. Yet, the chorus of those like them eventually drowns out all the other anguished voices.

We have seen this time and again. There is a public outcry. There are nominal changes in laws. There is increased awareness and a willingness to file a complaint.

Yet, you know and I know. Countless other women will be raped, killed, silenced, defaced with acid because as a nation, as a culture we glorify stalking. We believe women who are raped should be married to their rapists to save their reputations. We believe in staying in marriages that are abusive for God forbid, we walk out or what will the next door neighbor say?

The rot is inside, spread far and wide. What we need is not topical cleansing. We need a purge. We need a change in mindsets.

Until then, be afraid. Be very afraid.

It could have been you.

Today's song recommendation: Stronger - Kelly Clarkson

• • • • • • • • • • • •

Uma checks for spelling and grammar errors, tags her post and hits publish, feeling she has done what she can to process all that was churning inside her.

The unfairness of what had happened seems to bounce inside her, knocking on walls, skewing carefully positioned wall decor. She reflects on her relationship with Aditya. In the five years since she and Aditya have been married, they have fallen into an uneasy truce. Once she had wished and prayed to marry him. Once, she had pinned her dreams on him. The reality was so different from what she had imagined. Abuse does not have to be physical, does it? she wonders. Indifference and apathy are worse. Why do I not walk out? she asks herself.

These questions have been popping up inside her head at regular intervals over the past year. She had been telling herself to give it time. Aditya was not a bad guy. And she was not quite sure what was wrong. From a distance, he had seemed so perfect. Tall, dusky, and handsome, he was the son of family friends, someone she had known growing up. No hints or whispers of any scandal. School, college, grad school, a well-paying job. All the boxes her parents had listed were checked. Yet, here they were five years into their marriage, and she was not quite sure what was wrong and how to fix it. He just seemed to not care.

It had been the summer of 2007 when Aditya had finally agreed to marry Uma. She had broken up with her biker boyfriend earlier that year and had not particularly been thinking of marriage when her mom had suggested Aditya. Well, it was Aditya. The boy she had pined for all through school and college. She had said yes, unthinking.

Aditya and she had met. A formal meeting orchestrated by her parents and his. They had gone up to the terrace of her house while their parents caught up on gossip and traded jokes. Aditya had said something about having nightmares and being damaged. She had wondered if he was trying to scare her away. "Who doesn't, Aditya?" she had asked. "I come with enough baggage for the two of us."

She had stood on tiptoe and kissed him on his lips.

"Do you even like me?" she had asked, noting his stunned silence. He had looked at her, surprised, and shrugged. "What is there to like?" This is an arranged marriage. I do not know anything about you. I suspect we will learn as we go."

Her antennae had gone up. He had not reacted the way she had expected him to. She had wanted to ask, "What do you want from marriage?" but then wondered if the answer would change how she felt.. Realizing that it did not matter, she had gone full steam ahead. But she was regretting it now.

They had gone through the motions of marriage and settled down in Aditya's home in Austin. He was a US citizen. That meant she was eligible to work if she wanted to. She had debated between working and studying. Eventually she had decided on taking a break and getting to know Aditya first.

There was nothing in their relationship that she could point to and say, "Oh, this is what is wrong with us." It was like trying to put together a puzzle. Pieces that should have snapped together didn't. They fit the cutouts, but there was resistance, indicating perhaps that this was not the piece. They had different tastes in decor, in food, in books, on life.

Simply put, they were two left feet trying to dance together.

Uma had tried valiantly the first year. She had been annoyed the second year. She had tried to fight and get him to notice her the third. Then she had given up. They had sex all right. That was one area where they were compatible. He knew how to satisfy her. And she knew what made him come. So, under the cover of darkness, they became one and she pretended all was well in their marriage. Intimacy, though, was what she craved. Physical touches were a far cry from being seen, being loved, being held in tenderness. She feared that if they lost even the ability to make physical love, there would be nothing to connect them at all.

It is early afternoon. December in Austin is cold, if nothing like the snow-covered Northeast. On impulse Uma calls her cousin Devika and asks her if they could go out. She wants to get something for their trip to Philly this Wednesday. Her hosts' daughter Vibha is a tween and she wants to get her something that she would like.

Devika says she will pick her up. Uma dresses, leaves a note for Aditya at the kitchen island saying she will be late, locks up behind her and stands waiting for her cousin and a few hours of retail therapy.

———

ADITYA: ANATOMY OF A MARRIAGE

Aditya returns home to find it empty and relief sweeps over him. He texts Uma to find out when she will be home, gets changed and makes an early dinner of leftovers. He settles on the couch, beer in hand and turns the TV on. The Cowboys are playing the Eagles and he is reminded of Anand. Absently he looks at his phone and sees Uma has texted him back. "I am having dinner with Devika. She will drop me back on her way home. I have bought gifts for Rashmi, Anand and, Vibha."

He remembers with a start that they are flying out to Philadelphia in a couple of days. He has work in Philly and Rashmi had insisted that they stay the weekend and spend Christmas break with them. So he had booked tickets for Uma as well. She had been reluctant to cancel her plans with Devika and Bhaskar. He had not insisted but the next morning she had agreed.

His marriage to Uma is as much an enigma to him as it is to her. He had married her willingly, but almost as if to punish himself for not having been man enough for Sandhya. Had he hoped that he would eventually fall in love with her? In the five years since their wedding, he had alternated between loathing her for not being whom he wanted her to be and loathing himself for not being the kind of partner he wanted to be. He had been waiting for her to prod, to provoke, to make him man up. She had held back, waiting for him to grow up. He knew deep down he had to either change or let her go. But he had stayed passive, waiting for things to happen rather than initiating them. He does not hate her. He does not love her either.

The game resumes but his mind is not on it. He turns the TV off and reaches for his phone instead. His email shows two new messages. One is from an old classmate, Shankar, who is in the area and asking if he was free this weekend. Aditya quickly replies that he will be out of town. The other is from his brother, letting him know his plans for Philly have been cancelled because his kids are sick.

"Excuses!" Aditya mutters to himself as he pulls up Facebook. His timeline is flooded with holiday cheer and he is not quite sure why that annoys him. Skimming through his news feed he lands on a link petitioning for change to the rape laws in India. The word rape sends a shiver through him and he clicks on the link without being aware of doing so. There is a brief description of Nirbhaya's rape and why the rape laws in India are antiquated and need to be changed. He signs the petition and feels the cheer from the beer evaporate. It is dark outside and he has not switched on the lights inside.

His thoughts meander to Sandhya and eventually Vetri and Rajesh. Over the years he has perfected the art of pushing unwanted memories to the back of his brain. Now they only sneak in when he is unguarded, like when he is asleep or in the shower. Right now, he can feel the memories coming. The rush of images, replete with graphic detail of what he had seen. He squeezes his eyes tightly shut to drive these images away. He feels lonely. He has been lonely for a long while.

Uma enters, chatting gaily with Devika and carrying a lot of bags. He rushes to take them from her and switches on the light. Devika makes a comment about leaving the love birds alone and giggles as she walks away. He watches Uma's smile fade as Devika leaves. He is struck with sadness, for Uma, for himself.

He looks at her critically. Everything about her screams gaudy. He averts his eyes for fear of saying something. Realizing Uma has asked him something, he turns. "Did you have dinner?" she asks and he nods. Feeling compelled to respond, he asks, "What about you? Do you want me to heat something up for you?"

Something akin to hope flares in Uma and she smiles. "We did get something at the food court. She paid." She leaves the statement incomplete, hurrying to the center table and opening the bags. Aditya feels overwhelmed by the idea of discussing her purchases. Not quite sure what possesses him to be so rude, he says, "Please don't get started on your afternoon trip. I am not in the mood for this now."

Uma quietly packs everything back into their bags and walks upstairs. He feels bad but is not sure what to say. While it is true that he is not in the mood for a high energy account of her afternoon, could he have been kinder, he wonders.

He is exhausted by how he feels in his marriage. He had thought he had gone into it with an open mind. He had been wary of marrying a stranger, but Uma had seemed perfect. He had known her growing up, though from a distance. Her breakup had been public knowledge and it had gladdened him that he was not the only one bringing baggage to their new life together.

But things had gone wrong right from the wedding preparations. His parents had been content to let Uma run the show. He had envisioned a smaller wedding. Primarily people both families knew and a honeymoon in rural Kerala. But they ended up with a wedding where he had known fewer than a handful of the guests. There had been photo shoots prior to and after the wedding. He had protested wearing a sherwani but had been made to wear one anyway. They had honeymooned in Bali on a trip paid for by his father-in-law despite his objections.

When they had flown to Austin, he had hoped to reclaim the peace and quiet he had missed in the weeks leading up to the wedding. Instead, he had been invited into the wide circle of Uma's extended family who now considered him family as well. He had flailed and gasped for space. Since then, their marriage had progressively gone downhill. He had seen Uma encroach on his space physically and mentally. Unprepared, he had given way and ended up resenting her for it.

The irony was that Uma had had no clue how he had been feeling until a few years into their marriage when it had all come out in a vile vocal outburst. Uma had stood stunned and then withdrawn from him. They had arrived at an impasse that neither of them knew how to move on from. Separation and divorce had crossed his mind several times, but he had shelved the thought out of deference for their families. Instead, he had kept hoping that she would bring up the issue, but she had not either.

For someone who had aced his student and professional life, this failure had hit him hard. And he had succumbed to it by moving from disinterest to apathy.

———

UMA: OF LOST JOURNALS

Uma wakes up in the early hours of the morning and finds the bed empty. She tries to go back to sleep but gives up and brushes her teeth instead. Craving a cup of coffee, she finds Aditya slumped on the sofa and the TV still on. Turning the TV off, she prods Aditya and he goes upstairs to their bedroom.

Coffee mug in hand, she heads to the study and mulls opening the laptop. Then, realizing they must travel in a couple of days, she decides to get started on the packing. She goes to the storage and roots around for the bags they usually carry to India. Realizing they are too big for just a few days' stay; she looks around to find two other mid-sized cases tidily covered. Slipping the covers off, she hefts them outside. One seems a little heavy.

Instead of carrying it upstairs, she opens it to find a bunch of books inside. They are yellowing and look well read. She flips through them, surprised by Aditya's tastes. The subjects are eclectic. Buried almost at the bottom is a journal of sorts. She debates looking through it and decides that if Aditya did not deem it important enough to lock up, it is fair game. Also, she is curious. She slips the journal into the pocket of her housecoat, reminding herself to put it back after she is done reading it.

Remembering that Aditya is anal about his things, she decides disturbing the case with the books and puts it back where she found it. She grabs the empty suitcase and a couple of cabin-sized bags and lugs it all upstairs.

It is 5:00 am and she is mostly done with her bag. Excepting a couple of shirts she is not sure Aditya likes, she has packed his bag as well, the best she can. She figures the gifts can go in the third bag. Leaving it all zipped up and stacked in a corner, she decides to go for a run. After writing a note for Aditya, she steps out, the journal in her cross bag. She jogs slowly, making her way towards the park nearest their home. The streets are deserted and the sun is not out yet. But its early rays are breaking the horizon and the world around her is peaceful.

She jogs along the biking track and, curiosity getting the better of her, finds a bench to sit on to read the journal. The journal's cover is inscribed with the year 1996. He must have been in his last year of college then, she realizes, counting back from 2012. She skims through the diary. The entries are innocuous enough. They mostly seem to be thoughts on the books he is reading. Except for occasional references to a Sandhya who seems to share his love for books. A few entries catch Uma's attention. Aditya seems wistful, almost lonely. Her heart goes out to this stranger of a man she is married to. She skips passages and stops on one.

"I wonder what she sees in Surya. There is possessiveness in the way he watches her. I shouldn't be bothered, but I am…"

Intrigued, she scans through the rest of the entries, building an image of a man in love with a woman and having no intention of declaring it. Towards the end of the journal, the entries seem hopeful. It looks like the two of them were headed for grad school together. A few pages seem to be missing, some pages have ripped edges. The last entry reads:

"I am not sure what I am doing is right. I should have stuck around to see if she needed help. But seeing Surya there reminded me of my place in her life. On the flip side, I must have lost the bookmark she gave me. Is it a sign perhaps to let go?"

Uma closes the journal, trying to make sense of the boy that Aditya had been. He seems to have felt so much. He was a romantic at heart. Where did this person go? What had happened to Sandhya? Who was Sandhya? She is left with more questions than answers. She sits at the park until the sun is up and then walks home slowly, her mind turning over this new found knowledge in a bid to decipher the puzzle that is her life.

———————

ADITYA: DREDGING UP MEMORIES

The sun is bright when Aditya opens his eyes. He remembers falling asleep on the couch. Uma must have sent him upstairs though he is unable to recall when or how. Uma is nowhere to be seen or heard. He decides to shower and head down. Reaching the kitchen, he finds a note that says, Out for a run. You are on your own for breakfast and lunch.

This is unusual for Uma. He decides to make amends and roots around in the pantry. Finding a mason jar filled with aval, he chops up chilies, dices ginger and curry leaves and makes a quick breakfast of aval upma. He packs some away and leaves a note that says, I am sorry for being so brusque yesterday.

This is a first for him. He wonders if this is what he had been waiting for from Uma, a show of independence and assertiveness. He loves that she has decided to take off for a run and not baby him the way she usually does. He thinks he had told her so many times, but then wonders, other than occasional eruptions from both of them, had they ever had a conversation that went beyond the surface?

As he gets ready to leave, his phone pings with a message from his college classmate, Shankar.

"I'm in Austin today and tomorrow. Meet for lunch or dinner sometime?" Aditya hesitates a few seconds before typing back. "Today works. I will call you around 11:00 and we can pick a place."

Driving to work, his mind goes back to college and Shankar.

The auditorium where the counseling was held had been packed. Students and parents milled around, clutching mark sheets and important looking documents. His dad had accompanied him. They had been narrowing down their choices based on his score, hoping spots in Tier I colleges would still be left by the time his name was called.

He had gone up and been disappointed when his choices from around Madras had been taken. "Take Karuna," his dad had suggested. "Coimbatore is a nice place; the college has a good reputation. There is talk about it going autonomous. Given the state of our professors in the so-called Tier I colleges, it may be a good thing." Aditya had agreed. Partly because he could not care less if his college were not in Madras.

He had heard later from a friend that Sandhya was going to Karuna too and wondered if the fates were teasing him. When he had seen her at the station, he had felt a sense of peace about his decision claim him.

In Coimbatore, he had been pleasantly surprised by the lack of humidity. The station had been clean and the people seemed kinder than those in Madras. Anand had come to receive him and he had spent a few days walking about and exploring the city before college started.

The campus had looked intimidating with its gates wide open. He had noted the petty shop right by the entrance, the smell of cigarette smoke reaching him before anything else. Anand had seen him eyeing the shop and reminded him that it was no fun battling addiction. It was funny how much saner the same thing felt coming from a peer rather than a parent.

He had smiled, hefted his backpack, and strode right in. The entrance had been majestic, with pillars supporting a huge awning. He had walked up the steps, wondering how old the building was. The halls were wide, the classrooms airy and well lit. Each class had a small wooden dais for the professor. Each student had a desk and he was happy he wouldn't have to share a bench with anyone. He had picked a spot by the rear entrance to each of his classes as advised by Vetri, a classmate he had met on the train to Coimbatore. "Easier to slip out of," Vetri had winked.

The buildings formed a quadrangle, a grassy patch of land in the center. Students sat along the corridors, legs dangling off the ledge and over the grass. A few seniors lay in the sun, ordering their minions to embarrass themselves. He had hurried along, hoping to remain invisible.

The rear entrance had led down a few steps to a huge open-air stadium. There had been a canteen, a workshop for mechanical engineering students and lots of open land. The hostel buildings had risen in the distance, tall, dank, and bereft of adornment.

His room had been furnished sparsely with a steel cot and a table and chair. A ceiling fan whirred above him noisily, the regulator that controlled its speed broken. A single naked bulb hung low, emitting a mellow light that did not quite reach the floor. The other part of the room had a similar setup. His roommate was yet to come so Aditya had picked the bed nearer the window and set up his few belongings nearby.

The bathrooms and shower stalls had reflected the same sparseness.

The rooms had had high ceilings and he had felt dwarfed by it all, he recalls.

Before other unpleasant memories the ragging that had marked his first year at Karuna intrude, Aditya turns his thoughts to Shankar.

They had been classmates for four years. They hadn't been friends particularly, but then he had hung out with Vetri and Rajesh mostly. Shankar had gone to Ohio State while Aditya had been at Drexel. He had missed the only college reunion after grad school. What bothers Aditya is that Shankar is in touch with most of their class, including Vetri.

They end up meeting at Masala Wok, something of a desi hotspot in Austin. Over lunch, they catch up on their personal and professional lives. Aditya shares that he is married and has no kids yet. He wonders why he feels compelled to mention it.

Shankar had married their classmate Veena and they have two daughters. He brings up Rajesh and Vetri and mentions that they are both bachelors, looking at Aditya to gauge his reaction.

"Why?" Aditya asks, wondering if his past has finally stepped into the present.

"Didn't you know?" Shankar lowers his voice. "There were rumors…" he pauses and continues "…they were left at the entrance to their homes, all beaten and bloody." He pauses and in a dramatic whisper says, "Somebody castrated them that day. I wouldn't have known if not for a drunken brawl at the end of our last reunion. The one you missed."

Aditya realizes why Shankar has sought him out and wonders how he can get out of this conversation and get back to work. Shankar looks at him sharply and says:

"Most people suspected that either you or Surya had a hand in it, except you were with us at the hostel at that time and Vetri had seen Surya with his folks on his way to the old bus stop. How did you pull it off?"

The eagerness in his tone is sickening. Aditya thanks the stars that Shankar has not mentioned Sandhya and wonders if he can hit him and get away with it. . Before he can do that, Aditya gets up, flips Shankar the bird and walks out, dropping a $20 bill on the table for his share of the meal.

He wonders as he strides to his car if people like Shankar stop to realize that these are actual people's lives, he loves to gossip about. He wonders what Shankar and his ilk say about Sandhya and ironically realizes Surya had had it right. The best way to have dealt with the situation was to have kept it under wraps.

The drive back to work is short and fueled by an emotion he does not recognize. His hands tremble as he parks. He sits in the car for a long time before he gets out. His mind reels with the impact of what he had heard. For years he had beaten himself up for walking away and never looking back. Karma, he realizes is a bitch. He has never really stepped out the shadows of the past, has he?

SANDHYA: DREAMS AND DISQUIET

December 20, 2012

Malvern PA, USA

Everybody likes happy endings, right? I do. I am a sucker for love stories. There is this girl blogger I used to follow online. She calls herself The Sun Goddess. I mean, look at her pseudonym. Fabulous, right?

Yesterday, I caught up on her posts after a long time, more than five years, I think. I had started following her blog when I was in Bangalore, having stumbled on it from a comment she had left on one of my book reviews. I liked her writing style. She had snark and was irreverent. I love that in writing.

For years this girl had been silently in love with a friend of her family. He was much older than her and obviously, in the way that all crushes go, she got real when she entered college. Then she dated this guy who was a biker and a musician to boot. It had heartbreak written all over it. Her story read like a train wreck and when she crashed and burned, I stopped reading her. I grieved for her and for me. For what had been lost. Perhaps the hurt in her words had resonated with the pain in my heart. Maybe I had wanted to see her ride off into the sunset with her biker boyfriend, heading for a happy ever after.

Today, I don't know why, I looked her up after work and found that I had missed a lot. Quite a LOT! Turns out her story had a happy ending after all. In a strange turn of events, the guy she had crushed on all through school had agreed to marry her. Obviously, the match had been engineered by their parents, but she was not complaining. They got married and she moved to the US. She doesn't say where, but I think from now on I will be scanning any new Indian women I meet for her. Her latest blog mentions she is headed to the Northeast!

• • • • • • • • • • • •

Party!

We are off to the beautiful Northeast today. You know what that means, right? I will be off my blog for a while. I am hoping for a white Christmas and perhaps a new life in the new year.

Get your minds out of the gutter. I am mulling changes —small ones and big ones. Will clue you in when I am back.

Stay chill and happy. Merry Christmas and Happy New Year y'all!

xoxo!

The Sun Goddess

Song Recommendation: Deck the Halls with Boughs of Holly. :)

• • • • • • • • • • • •

Perhaps it is the effect of reading chick lit blogs before bed, but I wake with the feeling of a man nuzzling the back of my neck. I realize uncomfortably that I remember vivid details from my dream: a prominent Adam's apple and a bristly chin that had my skin prickling with need and my insides twisting with an unnamed feeling. Surprised that I had not woken up to blazing lights and Vikram rubbing my back, I look around and Vikram is on the other side of the bed, mouth open, snoring gently. There no prominent Adam's apple and his cheeks are as smooth as a baby's butt.

"Strange dream," I mutter to myself as I squeeze the paste on to my toothbrush and brush with a vigor that is unusual for me. As the foam works its way into the crevices of my mouth, I wonder why I had been dreaming about him. I mentally count back to 1997. Fourteen years! I had last seen him in the afternoon of my last day at college.

Feelings I have managed to keep at bay all these years threatens to overwhelm me. Inhale. Exhale. Inhale. Exhale. I repeat this to myself the way my therapist has taught me to. As the panic ebbs, I focus on each task as if my life depends on it.

I remember the day I first saw him. June 05, 1989, eighth grade, my first day at the new school. I had had to take the bus to get there. Appa had taken me the previous day to show me the route. I had walked in with trepidation. There was a quadrangle where a whole lot of kids were playing. Buildings enclosed the space. My classroom was on the third floor. I went to the administration office to find out where my classroom was exactly and was told to ask for Padma ma'am when I got there. Padma ma'am turned out to be a cherubic woman with kind eyes. She helped me find a spot near the center of the class and assured me I would find the class easy to get along with. I did not quite believe her, but was prepared to keep an open mind.

"Raise your hands if you are new," said the teacher and two hands went up, mine and his. He was tall for his age. He had oversized glasses set in a dark rectangular frame. There was fuzz on his upper lip and he had a prominent Adam's apple. His earnestness was marred by a twinkle in his eyes. I liked him.

We had moved homes from Adayar to the outskirts of the city, trading an apartment for a home with trees, a compound, and an open terrace. I had left behind my all-girls school where I had taken refuge behind the mass of pinafore clad girls trading identity for anonymity, and braved a new world of co-education.

The new school had smaller classes. And there were boys. The library was a good size compared to my old school. And most importantly, it had the full Nancy Drew collection I was then reading. I had found my happy place, my new refuge.

How many boys actually go to the library? Apparently one boy did. His name was Aditya. As I scanned the shelves for books I hadn't read before, he walked in with the ease of someone who knew what he wanted. I picked out the first book that had appealed to me before retreating to my corner, trying hard not to be aware of him. I remember the pungent smell of sweat as it moistened my underarms. I remember the swell of my nascent breasts as they pushed against my shirt.

Then there had been that time in English class. I had just finished an Irving Wallace book over the weekend. One I had no business reading in ninth grade. The phrase "cat in heat" had been burning a hole in my head. The dictionary did not help with phrases. The bell rang, the class dispersed and I sought out my English teacher. Then I noticed him out of the corner of my eye. He was lingering too. Hesitating, I almost made it to the door when the teacher called my name.

Looking around to make sure he was not listening, I whispered, "What does a cat in heat mean?" I remember that day like it was yesterday. The teacher considered my question with gravity and in her warm, level voice asked, "What have you been reading, Sandhya?" With all the naiveté of a child woman, I blurted out the name of the book and was relieved when she laughed and whispered what it meant. I remember turning a deep shade of pink and walking outside without looking at him.

I had gone home and pulled out my dictionary, learning words like copulation, fuck, and intercourse. My education was complete, I deemed.

Over the years, his frame filled out, his facial features became angular and he towered over the rest of the boys in the class. His voice lost the boyishness and became sonorous. We were in different sections and rarely acknowledged each other when we passed in the corridors. I always turned back to look at him if there was no one with me. His stride was long and I admired the way his muscles were outlined against his trousers as he walked like he owned the place.

I did not pass him my yearbook after the farewell party our juniors threw us. I did not say bye. I was on a train bound for college when I saw him again. He sat by the window seat a couple of coaches away from mine. He looked small and lost in the crowd that milled around the station. My parents and Usha stood with me, repeating instructions, and warning me about the perils of staying alone in a strange city.

Walking out of orientation on the first day of college, I bumped into him in the hallway, his tall frame against my petite one and we stood, an awkward silence filling the gap between us. The summer had tanned him and he looked ready for the world.

Over the four years of my undergrad, we settled on a friendship of sorts. We met in the library, checked books out, sat on the steps leading out and kept our discussions centered on books. He offered recommendations and I buried my obsession with regency romances and doled out names of books I thought he would like. I noticed he never approached me if he was with his group of friends. I was not sure if I minded that or not.

The last day of college, sure that we would be headed to the US together, I pulled out a shiny, tasseled bookmark engraved with his initials, A.R. for Aditya Raghavan, and gave it to him when we met at our usual haunt. I felt a warm pleasure flood my cheeks when he turned it over a few times and carefully tucked it into the journal he carried everywhere. In turn he handed me a second-hand copy of Roots by Alex Haley, mentioning that he thought I would learn more about the country I was headed to by reading it.

I thought that was the last time I had seen him except for the fact that I found the bookmark along with my belongings when I was discharged from the hospital on the last day of college. A day I try hard not to remember.

Unless you count the dream today that is.

———

ADITYA: OF BUTTERFLIES AND ARRANGED MARRIAGES

20 December, 2012

Wayne PA, USA

I wake up to the alarm trilling in my ear. For a moment I am not sure where I am. I turn and notice Uma sleeping beside me. Her face, scrubbed of make-up, is child-like. Her hair is splayed around her head almost like a halo. I am tempted to brush it away. To take a closer look at the woman who is my wife. Asleep, she seems approachable. I slip out of bed quietly, padding in my borrowed slippers into the bathroom. I close the door and turn the light on.

Rashmi has the bathroom stocked with the essentials I need. I leave the toilet kit in my suitcase and help myself to the guest supplies. I sit on the toilet, phone in hand, scanning my messages. I delete the one from Shankar without opening it. Putting the phone away, I look around. I have always been one for detail. I notice things most people do not. Like the tile on the floor that has been changed. The color difference hits me in the eye. The newer caulking is a giveaway. I notice if there is gunk on the shower curtain liner. I notice hair curling on the shower drain. I am compulsive like that, possibly a result of having lived alone most of my adult life. I am not sure why stereotypes about bachelors and apartments exist. Mine is spartan.

I admire Rashmi's taste in decor and the toiletries she stocks. I know it is Rashmi because Anand is a slob. I am an anomaly, I guess. I am also different because I talk to myself a lot. In my head, of course. Most people misinterpret my silence for arrogance or disinterest when it is neither. I cannot voice something if I do not understand it well myself.

A warm shower later, I am back in the bedroom digging for my clothes when Uma wakes. I make a mental promise to be nicer to her. She looks at me and points to the other suitcase, indicating that my clothes are in there. I thank her and get dressed as she watches. She goes back to sleep as I head downstairs for a cup of coffee before I leave for work.

My cousin Anand and niece Vibha are at the island with steaming mugs of coffee. I pour myself a cup and walk over as Anand gets up and gives me the one-armed hug that we have perfected over the years. "Good to see you, man!" he says heartily and I feel included and at home. Anand and I go back many years. He is my first cousin, my dad's brother's son. I spent every summer of my growing up years with his family near Peelamedu in Coimbatore. I have very fond memories of those times. Coimbatore is nestled in the foothills of the Nilgiri mountains. Each morning we would go up to the flat terrace of their house to fly kites. I have vivid memories of the blue-tinged mountains silhouetted against a clear sky.

We catch up on family as his wife Rashmi joins us.

"Isn't Uma up yet? I was hoping to get to know her before I log in to work," she says, looking around as if Uma might pop up before she finishes her sentence. . "I know," I say half-heartedly. Rashmi looks at me as if expecting more. "She's had a rough night. Didn't sleep until early morning. She will be down in a bit." Rashmi exchanges a look with Anand and sets cereal, milk, and bread out on the island.

"We really wanted to make it to the wedding, you know?" Rashmi says, looking at me earnestly. "We had given up on you ever getting married! So how did it happen, Aditya? You owe us the full story." She winks at me. I smile naturally and try to deflect.

Rashmi is one of those people who hates silences. She rushes in to fill awkward spaces with chatter before anyone can notice, as if the void will balloon and none of us will be left with anything to say. Before she can bring Uma up in conversation, I turn my attention to Vibha.

I do better with children than I do with adults. I ask her about what she is reading and we get into an animated discussion about books. She says she is midway through the Harry Potter series so we go back and forth on each character and she leaves for school with a smile. I envy her reading the series for the first time. In fact, sometimes I think I would give anything to go back and reset my life from high school.

The warm buzz I felt evaporates with Vibha's departure. Anand and Rashmi are pottering around the kitchen with the ease of two people wordlessly in sync. Often, I wonder what would have happened if the last day of college had been different. Would I have had a life with Sandhya by my side?

I think about Sandhya a lot. I think about what happened after she was raped. I think of the part I played in it. I think about a lot of things. And these things are not conducive for happy, normal relationships. In the aftermath of that day, I could never see women the same way.

To be specific, I could never look at a woman below her neck without images of scratches and blood haunting me. I am uncomfortable around cleavage and will go to any length to avoid being in such situations. They say time heals. I say time deadens, dulls, and rubs out the sharp images. But memories never really go away, do they?

I have a brother. Ashwin. He is everything I am not. Whole, untouched by tragedy. He followed the arc I should have. School, college, grad school, job, marriage, kids and now the suburban home with a fence and a dog. I have never really told anyone in my family about Sandhya, about that night, except for Anand. He knew because he showed up at the college to pick me up and I was not there. He is the closest thing I have to a friend.

I married Uma because I eventually ran out of reasons to not marry. Uma's parents and my parents have been friends from the cradle, as they like to remind us. I saw her grow up. I do not know what she thinks of me. She is a good five years younger than me.

Uma reminds most people of a butterfly. She flits in and out of rooms, filling them with light and beauty. Fleeting, elusive beauty.

I tried to talk her out of the marriage. I tried to tell her I was damaged. I had started to talk about my nightmares when she had stood up on tiptoe, pressed her lips against mine and shushed me.

"I have known you since I was born, Aditya!" she had laughed. "I have always loved you."

What does one say to that kind of a declaration?

We had married a month from the day that the idea of a marriage between the two of us had been broached. Two weeks later, we had set up home in suburban Austin. I had nightmares on my side of the bed and she cried herself to sleep on the other side.

Perhaps my eyes have glazed over. Anand coughs and intrudes into my thoughts with a reflective, "So, you taking up the offer to move up here?"

Grateful for a reprieve from the unpleasant thoughts in my head, I answer with alacrity.

"I am considering it, Anand. It is a good move. I will be handling a larger set of regions. Plus, it will put me in the financial hub and open other opportunities career wise."

I pause and punt the question back to him. "What do you think?"

As Anand wraps up all the advantages of moving closer to him, I realize I will have to leave for work now or risk missing the train. I have visited him many times, but still prefer taking the train to navigating Philly traffic in the morning. I rinse my coffee cup at the sink and leave it on the drain board.

"Rashmi will appreciate that," Anand laughs and I walk upstairs to wake Uma and grab my laptop bag. She is awake when I walk in, sitting in front of the mirror and brushing her hair. A change of clothes is set on the vanity. I nod approvingly and on impulse reach out to take her hand.

"You will be okay. Anand and Rashmi are nice. I will be back tomorrow evening."

I walk out leaving several things I want to say unsaid. Perhaps it was watching Anand and Rashmi, but I feel I should make more of an effort to reach out. I sling the bag across my shoulder and look up directions to the train station as I walk to the car.

Carefully backing out of the driveway, I catch Anand in my rearview and wave as I leave. The development he lives in is one of the older neighborhoods. One acre lots with smaller houses. The lawns are mowed and edges trimmed and the trees are mature. Swing sets dot the backyards and scooters and bikes line the driveways. I take in these tiny details as I merge into the county road and make my way to the station.

The morning is cold and I tug my jacket closer as I walk up the steps, a strong wind pushing me back. I pay for a ticket to Suburban station and sit down to wait on a bench with a copy of the Philadelphia Inquirer. I scan the pages and settle on the sports page. I may have moved away from Philly since grad school, but I still cheer for the Eagles.

The station has a fair amount of people waiting to board. Students, commuters working in the city and the odd tourist. I feel a kinship with these people. They remind me of streams joining together as they empty into a river. A confluence of folks converging on the city. I hear the rumble of the train in the distance and get up.

I get onto the first compartment I can and find a spot near the entrance. As I settle down, I glance up and see her. I am startled. I cannot seem to take my eyes off her. She is radiant. She reminds me a sunflower, cheerful, arrogant, and happy. For years, I have imagined running into her on my India trips. The last I had heard from common friends, she lived and worked in Bangalore. Realizing she had not recognized me, at least not immediately, I turn my attention to the paper and raise it to cover my face. My mind however, is reeling.

She has been in my thoughts constantly for over fourteen years now. Yet, here she is, in flesh and blood and I am flummoxed. Common sense tells me I should put the paper down, give her time to recognize me and then introduce myself. But I am not sure I am ready for that.

I am tempted to look up, to see what may be running through her mind. I slip my shades on, lower the paper, and see she is reading Gone Girl. At least I know now that she is still the same reader she has been. I am not sure what I had expected to see if I ever saw her again.

Someone broken? I look at her again. She looks the same as I remember her being, but for subtle changes. Her hair, neatly tied, shows traces of grey at the roots. Her usual dangling earrings have been replaced by solid diamonds winking in the sun. Crow's feet line her eyes. I can see laugh lines on her face. Her eyes are wary but bright. She seems to blend in with the office-going crowd on the train. She is in business casuals and is carrying a laptop. There is not a trace of makeup on her apart from lip gloss. She looks good. I raise my paper again before I am caught staring.

———

UMA: UNDERSTANDING ADITYA

I delay getting dressed and going down. This is my first time in a house full of strangers. Technically, they are not strangers. These are names I heard all through my college years from Aditya's mom. I spent a lot of time with Mami and she often spoke about Anand, Adi's cousin who lived in Coimbatore and later moved to the US. It is strange visiting someone I had heard about all my life while growing up but never met. I gather the gifts I have for them and walk down. There is no one in the kitchen. It feels awkward and I pause, wondering if I should call out or walk around the house to find someone. As I stand there, Anand comes in from the front door. He radiates cheer.

"Anand," he holds out his hand. I put one of the packages down and take it. He is warm and friendly. I like him already. He leads me to the kitchen where I hold out the bag containing NFL stuff. I hope he likes it. He opens it and lets out a whoop of joy, making me happy. Rashmi comes in from the back patio. Her face is flushed from being out in the cold. She is a few years older than I am. She reaches out to me, arms extended for a hug, wraps me in a heartfelt squeeze and lets go. I feel welcome. I hand her gift. A set of nesting baking bowls I had found at a Williams Sonoma outlet. She seems genuinely pleased and accepts it graciously. I leave Vibha's gift on the island.

Rashmi sets a steaming mug of coffee in front of me and asks if I would like biscuits to dip in it. I refuse and she laughs. I sip the coffee and it warms me up.

"So, did you find everything okay? Let me know if you need towels, sheets, or toiletries. I can bring them up."

"Thank you. I have everything I need." I look around the house appreciatively. "You have a lovely house."

"Thank you," she says, beaming with pride. "You haven't met Vibha yet. She is a good kid."

"Aditya talks about her all the time," I say.

"So, how do you like Austin? I hear you have a huge extended family there."

I nod and as I am about to answer, she goes on.

"Guess that's why he is not considering moving here, is it?"

I look at her blankly. This is the first I am hearing of such a thing. "We haven't decided yet," I say after a pause. It hits me that they know something I do not. I turn it over in my head like a curiosity I find on my walk. It does not make sense. I know Anand and Aditya are close, but to exclude me in something as important as this? I stay silent.

I think Rashmi realized she said something she shouldn't have, so she comes over and stands beside me. I can feel tears welling up in my eyes. The strain of the past few years is beginning to show. I drain my coffee, excuse myself and go to the stairs.

"I'll talk to my mother, reply to emails and come back," I say as I go.

"I'll be working in the study if you need me," she says.

I sit at the edge of the bed, wondering what to make of her comment about Aditya refusing to move here. She had said it as though it was something that had been offered and he had refused. Should I be glad that he rejected something because I wouldn't have to move away from people I know? Anger builds on top of my feeling of helplessness. There is so much I don't know.

• • • • • • • • • • • •

Clueless

What do you do if the person you have been living with for five years is a stranger? You think you know them, but you don't. You stumble on relics from their past that indicate there is a lot behind the silent persona, but you cannot ask. You are in a house full of strangers and they seem to know more about your life than you do.

I am lost. Lost and lonely.

The Sun Goddess

• • • • • • • • • • • •

I call my mother on impulse and find out she is at Aditya's home. I hang up after a brief conversation. Turns out Ashwin and family are not coming to Philly. Suddenly the idea of spending the next four days with people I do not know seems tedious. A part of me is still mulling over the journal I had read the previous day.

I look back on all the years I spent pining for him. The happiness at discovering I was going to marry him. All the planning only to realize later that he had hated it all. The preparations, the photo shoots, the clothes. I look at myself sadly. It feels like this is a battle that will have no winner.

Images from the past five years flash before my eyes. The constant need for approval, the subtle put downs, the perennial feeling of not measuring up. I look at how much of my confidence all this has eroded. I was a successful career woman in Bangalore. I wonder why I quit and decided to take a break. In the years waiting for things to change, I could have started to build a future for myself. Perhaps if I had gone to work instead of trying to make the marriage work, walking out would have seemed possible.

I sit motionless, light breaking through the fog in my head. Even if not separation or divorce, I need to let go of the idea that I need him so that I can be happy. I should be out there doing the things that I love.

Suddenly it occurs to me that I have no clue what I am waiting for. I am 32. I have been married for five years. I haven't walked out on my husband. I am not considering separation. I am still on birth control. Thank goodness for that! The one time my period had been late had been a wake-up call. I'd known I couldn't bring a child into this family unless I was sure of my place there.

Life seems to be speeding past me while I am stuck in a rut.

———

SANDHYA: OF ANIMAL LOVERS AND THE AMERICAN DREAM

I am at the Paoli station. My iPhone shows today's high as 38F. I tap my feet impatiently as I wait for the lady before me to finish paying for her ticket in quarters. I feel goosebumps on my skin each time the door opens and a draft blows in. For all the years I have been here, I have never gotten used to the cold. I pull my cardigan closer and shift my weight from foot to foot to keep myself moving. I pay for my return trip ticket and step out of the cozy waiting room to the platform.

As I close the door behind me, I catch my reflection in the window pane. Blue pants, red blouse and an off-white cardigan with black edging. I look like the American flag!

The thought makes me want to laugh. The messenger bag with the laptop is slung across my shoulder. My hair is tied back in a neat ponytail and I am wearing a strand of pearls. I am almost tempted to check if my teeth are okay and then realize this is a window. I check the time again and realize I have fifteen minutes to kill before the train arrives. I could go back inside to the warmth but phone conversations, however low you try to keep your voice , tend to be amplified inside that confined space. It's too early to call my sister on the other coast, I realize. I text her to ping me when she is awake and dig in my purse for the copy of Gone Girl by Gillian Flynn. As I pull it out, I feel the phone buzz.

"Ping!" reads the text. I smile. Usha has a silly side to her that I adore.

"You awake this early? You are nuts!" I say.

"Let me call you," she says. I imagine Ishaan and Aravind fast asleep and Usha sneaking out to make a call.

The phone rings and I pick it up, my eyes dancing.

Usha is two years' older than me. Growing up, we were close, but after marriage we have been even closer. For a period following the assault at college, I had distanced myself from her. Between her, my mom, and my dad, we each had had different opinions on what should have been done. Usha, married and settled in the US at that time, was pushing for action, desperate to see the rapists behind bars. I had agreed with her but was angry that she could sit miles away from me and dictate what I should have been doing. So I had taken out my anger on her.

"You were not the one who was raped, right?" I had spat at her, the venom finding its mark. She had retreated into a shell, grieving from a distance.

It was Amma who had served as a bridge between the two of us, translating both her concern and my fears into the language of affection. Eventually we had agreed not to talk about it. She had pushed for me to accept my fellowship offer from Villanova and move here. But I had deferred my admission because I worried about being alone and helpless, waking from a nightmare with no one to turn to. In hindsight, the one year I had spent on therapy and preparing to move to Bangalore had helped. The therapist had been approachable, undemanding, and willing to work with me at my pace. Eventually, the one thing she kept circling around was that I had not been to blame.

"Why me?" had been my constant refrain. Would they have attacked me if I had not been Aditya's friend? Would they have spared me had I dressed differently?

It had taken me years to let go of the 'why me' and focus on the fact that my presence there had been incidental. There was no reason, no explanation for what had happened to me. All that was left was for me to pick up the pieces and choose how to respond to what had happened.

I shake myself from the deep thoughts I have sunk into at the sound of Usha's voice.

"Why are you up so early?" I ask, ready for some tale involving my nephew Ishaan.

"You know Ishaan, right? If there is a project due for school the next day, he tells me at 10:00 pm the night before and then shrugs it off, saying it's okay, Amma. I will manage. What is he going to manage? This boy will be the death of me!"

I laugh and she continues, "I have been up since 4:00 am trying to find out how to make lava for his volcano project." She sighs deeply. "So how is your glorious kid-free existence?"

I would have been offended if anyone else had said that, but I know Usha means no malice.

"Glorious!" I say. "By the way, are you still following TheSunGoddess?"

"Of course! Isn't it wonderful she got her Mister to marry her after all?" Usha sounds blissful as she imagines the story in her head.

"Why did you not tell me? I stopped following her after the biker guy broke her heart." I am miffed that my own sister would do this to me.

"How was I supposed to know you stopped following her? In any case, catching up on all that you missed should make for a nice lunch break read," she says.

I nod and notice the platform getting busy. I hear the train before I see it.

"Okay, I've got to go now. Talk to you on the weekend. Love to Ishaan. Bye!"

I hang up before she is done, clambering into the coach nearest me and settling down near a window. I pull out my book and continue from where I had left it the previous day. The next couple of stations fly past. "Coming up: Wayne," announces the disembodied voice over the speaker. I remember the party invite from Rashmi and wonder if she would mind if I cancelled on her. I do this all the time. I accept invites, sign up for events and when it is time to go, I wish I could backtrack or that the event will be cancelled.

The train lurches as it starts from the station. I glance up briefly as I turn the page, nodding my head as people pass by. As I return to my book, my eyes meet those of the passenger settling into the seat across from me and I feel a prick of unease. Something about him seems familiar. Perhaps my staring unsettles him. He raises his paper to block his face. I go back to my book but I am compelled to look up each time I pause between paragraphs. I give up, close the book, and settle back. He has the Philadelphia Inquirer open. A laptop bag lies across his lap and a pair of reading glasses is tucked into a side pocket. I am tempted to tap his paper and make him lower it. An image from my dream flashes before my eyes.

Aditya?

Could it be him? Here of all places? I want to laugh. I take in what I can see of him. The height seems about right.

He looks stockier than the Aditya I remember. The business suit looks expensive. I see a gold band on his ring finger. A Bluetooth earpiece blinks in his ear.

I wish he would lower the paper.

I look out the window. Mainline Philadelphia flashes by. The end of fall and early winter are usually beautiful. The days are short and the air cold. I love the hint of snow in the air. The bare trees look stark against the brilliant blue skies. School is in session and the buses are a yellow blur as the train hurtles to the next stop. Radnor, reads the signboard. I consider picking up the book again but my phone buzzes and I pull it out instead. I cannot seem to resist glancing at the man across from me. His hair is grey and silver. He has it cropped short. I wish he would lower the paper.

"Have fun in the city. Ace your presentation. Love you." It's Vikram.

I am smiling as I reply. The man does that to me. Twelve years into our marriage, he still surprises me with these notes. I wonder what he saw in me. I wonder what he still sees in me.

The trees are a blur as the train speeds towards the city. I had been married in October. The skies had been overcast and my parents had worried that guests might not make it if the hurricane hit. Me? I reveled in the rain. The torrential downpours that deluge Madras a few months a year. After months of relentless, humid heat, the rains are a respite, a welcome cleansing.

I was twenty-four. Ripe for marriage as my mom had put it. But then, I'd had a history. A blank space in my head where I should have known what happened to me on May 16, 1997. All I knew was that I had been found broken. Like a bird with its wings clipped. I had been clawed and violated. Not raped, they had repeated. All of them - Surya, Vennila, the doctor, the nurse, the college officials with whom I had insisted on filing a complaint, all of them had stonewalled me. They had denied me my victimhood. "You weren't raped," they said. "It was an accident. You fell and hurt yourself."

I had bumbled through the days after the assault, the not rape. My parents had driven in from Madras and had agreed with relief that I had not been raped.

Mom had sat beside me. Her hand warm against mine. Our shoulders side by side, like soldiers on parade. "Kettu poita nu solluva (They'll say she is damaged)," she had said. Tears had formed rivulets down her talcum-coated cheeks. Coimbatore is a small town, she had said. A small town with a small mentality. They will whisper, their whispers more insidious than anything shouted from the rooftops. They care about reputations. They care about protecting their own.

"Kettu poita." The word echoed in my head. I felt damaged. Spoilt, rotten, damaged. A bad apple, one with crawling maggots beneath the skin.

What she had left unsaid was this: This is what I have been trying to protect from your whole life. Our angst-filled fights, the 8:00 pm curfew, the injunction against talking or meeting with boys without an adult in the room. All those things had stemmed from a base fear. A fear that you would be raped, that you would be pilloried. Of having your name besmirched and reputation tarnished. My parents, my friends, the college authorities, the doctors at the hospital... no one said anything about the perpetrators. Boys will be boys and girls will have to be invisible. The onus to keep myself safe, I learned at long last, was on my shoulders alone.

Mom had cried. I had cried. We wept against the injustice and packed up, never to return. We could fight them, Sandhya, she had told me. But all that will happen is that they will drag your name through mud and then walk scot-free. It will be us against the system. She had looked so fragile and bent with sadness that I had given up.

Perhaps the not-rape had been a catalyst. All through college, mom and dad had urged me to do well, always adding as a caveat that I could study outside India if I agreed to focus on my studies and get a fellowship. I had agreed, like any good Indian girl would. Then everything had changed. They had encouraged me to pursue my dreams, to sprout wings and fly, to go on and conquer the world. Then, they pitied me because I had no clue what my dreams were now.

I opted instead to move out, took the train to Bangalore and joined the hordes of single, driven women out to conquer the tech world. I muffled my fears in my pillow at night. I carried pepper spray. I signed up to learn karate. And I avoided men. I avoided being around them. I avoided being with them.

My standoffishness was a candle, drawing men like moths. They arrived in droves and fell away singed and burned. My strategy had worked until Vikram.

His parents had called mine. Apparently, my mom had registered my natal chart with the local temple.

"Vikram Vaidhyanathan. Veterinarian."

Intrigued, I had read through the short bio and been impressed.

We had met, his eyes boring into mine over dinner. I had started with the easy topics. Work, dreams, philosophy. Then I talked about the rape. He had listened, not interrupting, not probing. He had waited until I was done and only then asked how I felt, if I had talked to a therapist. From there, he had transitioned to work and what I wanted to do with my life. His calm demeanor, his candid admission of how he still hated his late father for how the man had treated his mother and his guilt at not being able to do anything about it all seemed to explain why he was different from the other men I had met. He cared deeply for his mother, but clearly it stemmed from a place of empathy that extended to all things vulnerable. I instinctively felt I could trust him. He wanted to marry me. And I said yes. I have never had a reason to regret it.

A voice over the intercom announces the next station and I wake with a start. I gather my things and notice the man across from the seat doing the same. "First Private Bank" reads the monogrammed bag. I look up and he has his shades on. I look away.

I work for First Financial Bank. I have been working there for eleven of the twelve years I have been in the US. I worked my way up, switching from the technical to the business side and straddling both worlds with ease. I am a product manager with the bank and today I am presenting at a two-day conference meant for the management of the two banks to determine the course ahead for the merged entity.

Vikram is proud of me. I do not think he ever expected me to have a career. I am not being malicious when I say that. It is just the way he is. I do not think he ever mulls over anything other than what is concerning him at the present. When I applied to work at a bank, his raised eyebrow had said everything. He ferried me to and from work without complaints. As I moved up and eventually learned to drive, he seemed relieved to let me go. If I do not keep him abreast of what I do at work, I suspect he will not ask. It used to bother me initially when he did not ask about my work day or seem to care when my boss said something appreciative about my work. But he tried to explain that he honestly never thought beyond the now. I do not think I understood it then, but over time, I began to realize that this is who he is. He is a person who truly lives in the present, never concerned about material things like promotions at work or the creative high of a well-received book review. In any case, it is impossible for people to be perfect. Since Vikram must be imperfect in some way, I am glad that his imperfection is just this.

I enjoy being up early, packing lunches and leaving notes in his box. I get back early and prepare fresh food for dinner and the next day's lunch. He sees to the cleaning and what I call the paper trail. Bills to be paid, invoices to be filed and anything else that needs to be taken care of. We pay our mortgage on time, have no outstanding debts and decent savings in the bank.

Life is good. I am living the American dream. A double income, single-family home in the suburbs, complete with the white picket fence. Vikram and I have settled into a routine that is comfortable and safe. He has learned to accept my quirks and I have embraced his staid nature.

All we lack is a child. I brush away the thought before it threatens to overwhelm me. The train slows to a stop and I snap out of my reverie.

Getting off the train, I make my way along the platform to the stairs that spit passengers up the sidewalk. Merging into the tide of commuters that carries me along, I am surprised to see the man from the train next to me. His eyes look into mine like he is searching their depths for someone he knows. Before I can ask his name, we reach the sidewalk and I run to cross the road before the lights change. Gasping for breath, I stop on the opposite side and see him disappear into the sea of humanity that is Philly on a work day morning.

———

ADITYA: OF SORDID PASTS

I find a spot at a booth at the back of the cafe, settling in with my laptop. I put the paper away, folding it along the creases, but one sheet is out of sync and I cannot make myself let it go. I fold and refold, my mind still dealing with the implications of seeing Sandhya.

Fuck.

I would know her anywhere. I think she recognized me too. I am not sure I am ready to face her yet.

Fuck.

I gulp down my coffee and reach for the bagel. The phone buzzes. "Uma," flashes the caller id. I consider letting the call go to voicemail. Instead, I answer it and let my irritation show.

"I will be in meetings all day. I will call you when I can."

Before I can tell her not to call me till the work day has ended, she says something that gives me pause. "Rashmi said something about you considering a move to Philly. I did not know about it. It bothers me. I need to know, Aditya."

I feel a headache coming on. "We can talk about it tonight, Uma. It is not important. I do not have to decide right now. I need to go now. I promise we will talk about it."

I hang up before she can question me further. I wonder why I had never thought it important to ask her what she felt about the offer I had received. I finish my coffee and check my watch. I have a good one hour before the meetings start.

I put my phone away and open the laptop.

There are twenty odd unread email messages since I last checked in the morning. I scroll through them, filtering, marking, and prioritizing the ones I need to respond to.

'Amma' reads the sender of the last email. I smile as I open it. The email is short.

Aditya kanna,

Did you reach Philly safely? How are Anand, Rashmi, and Vibha kutty? Did you and Uma take gifts for them? I hope you did. Actually, I am sure Uma would have. You are lucky to have her. I hope we will hear some good news soon. I am praying for you daily.

Kochukaadhe, kanna. Summa dhaan sonnen (Don't be angry. Just kidding)!

Love,

Amma

———————

Amma,

Yes, I reached safely. Uma did get gifts for them all. Call you weekend.

Love,

Aditya

———————

I think of the pile of gifts Uma had bought earlier in the week. Suddenly, all my actions towards her seem heartless. My headache gets worse.

The momentum of the morning is lost and my thoughts stray to Uma. Pictures of her flash before my eyes. Uma of the pigtails, Uma of the gawky teenager phase, Uma who is painfully younger than me.

I had never paid particular attention to her, growing up. My mother had doted on her. Perhaps to make up for not having a daughter. I had seen her on my monthly visits home from college. Her curly hair framing her face and the dimples that deepened when she smiled. She had seemed perennially shy and I had been too interested in Sandhya then to pay any attention to her.

After college, I ran into her on my yearly visits. She had morphed into a petite, pretty girl. Whenever I saw her, she had had a phone glued to an ear and was given to giggling fits. I avoided her as much as possible.

I had heard from my mom that she had been in a relationship that she had walked out of. "He raised her hand at her," she had whispered. "Nalla ponnu. Paavam (Poor little good girl)." I am sure my mom had wanted to give me details, but I had stalled the conversation.

As I neared the age of thirty, Amma had demanded to see my boyfriend, convinced I was gay. "I will be happy for you, kanna, if you are happy," she had said, tears streaming down her face. No amount of denying that I had no partners of either gender worked. "If you are not in love, why will you not get married?" she had sobbed. I gave in. A month later, Uma and I were married and flying to Austin.

On our honeymoon, I had wanted to take the time to know her, to figure out this person I had married. I longed for slow-paced days by the pool or at the beach. But the woman I found myself with seemed high on life. She was excited enough for the two of us put together. She had each day planned out, with activities starting from daybreak to late night. I had tagged along, unwilling to rock the boat so early on. She had been big on gestures. I hated gestures big or small. She had been all hearts and candy. I was stark grey. She had believed that love conquers all. I was traumatized by it. Six months later, I was already mulling a separation, though I kept hoping she would be the one to bring it up. If she had thought about it too, I did never know. Her energy had never flagged. Only lately had she had become quieter, letting her hurt show.

The ding of an incoming mail brings me back to reality. 'Agenda' reads the title. I click open the attachment. My presentation is right before lunch. "Great!" I tell myself wryly and scan the rest.

"Sandhya Jayaraman - Proliant Demo" reads the last but one entry for the day.

I leave for the office with time to spare. The city is bustling with people marching with purpose. The day looks drab, the sun hidden behind gray clouds. Too early for snow, I think. Wisps of steam escape from grates. I walk at a brisk pace and reach the towering building on Market Street.

I check in and take the visitor badge I am offered. Slinging my laptop bag behind me, I join the queue for the elevators. Today's meetings are at the largest conference room in this building. I step on the plush carpet and feel right at home.

The room is large. Tables are clustered towards the sides, leaving the center open for demonstrations and for presenters to walk around. I spy copies of the day's agenda on each table. I pick one up and read it again, smiling at the entry 'Aditya Raghavan - A Merging of Cultures'. I seek Sandhya's name. Maybe I had imagined it, I think hopefully. But there it is. Sandhya Jayaraman - Proliant - Product Demo reads the line. I put the paper away and pick it up again, an uneasy feeling prickling at the back of my neck.

Sandhya.

I think of the woman I saw on the train and know that the name cannot be coincidental.

She had been J. Sandhya at school. For years, I had kept the memories at bay, but now there seems no escape. I take a sip of the lukewarm coffee I had poured myself at the door and walk towards the presenter's desk. Years of work-related travel have made me familiar with all conference rooms. I eye the microphone. I trace the wires and see they are plugged in. I check the view from the desk. Pleased with what I see, I walk back to my table.

With minutes to go before the first presentation, the room suddenly feels crowded. There are four other people at my table. I smile at my new colleague from the local office and we pump hands across the table. I look at the other three and introduce myself. We settle down and hear the screech from the mic as someone tests it.

I look up and freeze.

"Mic testing!" she says and smiles. A couple of people hoot from behind me and she waves. It is apparent that she is a familiar face here.

here. She walks away from the desk, all feminine grace and purpose. I pick up the agenda again. She is presenting towards the end of the day. I lean across to my colleague and ask if he knows her.

"Sandy?" She is an old hand. Knows her stuff," he says and glances around as if looking for her. He turns towards me and asks with interest, "Why do you ask?"

"I think I may know her," I say, weighing my words carefully. "We were in school together, I think."

"Small world, huh?" he remarks and grabs a copy of the agenda from the table.

There is rustling from near the microphone and everyone turns around. The organizer introduces himself and runs through the program. I tune out and let my mind wander.

It has been fourteen years.

The last time I saw her was in semi darkness. She had been propped against a brick wall, assaulted, kurta ripped and nail marks on her throat. I had stayed until her friends arrived. That evening has haunted me since.

Her assailants had been my friends. At least they had claimed to be.

I had met them on the train to Coimbatore. I was leaving Madras, my hometown, the city of bustling crowds, beaches, and throbbing markets. I had spent the last weeks of summer before college roaming the streets on my Yamaha bike. Hanging out with friends, knowing we were all headed toward different futures. Not one person from my school was going to the same place I was. Except for Sandhya. Sandhya, whose smile was imprinted on my brain.

My teenage crush on her had been my secret. One I shared with no one. I had haunted the library at school just so I could see her. In the end, I had taken to books as well and there had been no looking back.

On the train from Madras to Coimbatore, I had arrived early, settled myself in a corner seat and watched as kids my age walked past, bulky bags and labeled suitcases giving them away. I had seen Sandhya with her sister and parents a couple of coaches away, laughing under the light of the moth-ringed lamp post. Her hair had been like a halo around her face. I had been staring at her when the sound of a bag being dropped by my leg had brought me back to reality with a bang.

"Vetri," he had said, thrusting his hand toward me. All I could see was his Swatch and his Pepe jeans. "Aditya," I had countered, edging the book I was reading out of view. He had sat down next to me and introduced me to the boy next to him. "Rajesh," the boy had said, extending a sweat-lined palm.

By the time the train had rattled into Arakonam, we had traded GPAs, majors and realized we would be classmates. We exchanged numbers and hoisted ourselves on to our berths as the train rattled into the night.

Ours had been an unlikely partnership, born out of a need for survival. Ragging at Karuna Institute of Technology had the dubious distinction of being among the worst in the state. Whispers had made their rounds during the admissions process as nervous freshers shared tales that made my blood curl. I had been loath to admit to my dad that I was scared. So I had had my game face on, hoping the rumors were false.

But the truth was stranger than fiction. I was broken by the end of the first month. Just when I'd begun to consider running home, Vetri had taken me under his wing. His uncle was the college principal and he exuded the authority that family wealth and power had conferred on him. I had owed him. And he had extracted his pound of flesh the day he violated Sandhya.

Sandhya had remained in the periphery during our years in college. We acknowledged each other, but maintained a distance afforded by our connected past. I loved her. I loved the idea of her. A kindred soul and, a lover of books. I had watched her from a distance, falling in love with her spirited debates, with her ability to light up a room with just her presence. Over the first year of college, she had morphed from a caterpillar into a butterfly.

I had morphed too. Into a person I no longer knew. I had adopted the swagger of the clique. I took to booze initially to dull the pain and eventually because fuck, what else would I do each evening?

I passed her often on the steps of the library, surrounded by her coterie. She would occasionally follow me inside. We shared silences as we sat at adjacent tables, lost in our books. Sometimes I would walk her to her hostel. We would talk of school, of the people we knew, and wonder what the future held.

I had taken to reading under the cover of darkness just so I would have something to talk to her about. By then, she had found her group. She was their sun and they orbited her. The first time I saw her sitting with Surya in his car, I had been surprised by the mercurial rise of an unnamed emotion that threatened to overwhelm me. I retaliated by avoiding her altogether.

We shared a class in our final year and established a comfortable friendship. We met for the occasional coffee at the canteen and traded secondhand books. We joked about professors and exchanged notes on TOEFL and GRE. We applied to the same colleges and I hoped that perhaps we would be headed into the same future.

We had met on the last day of college. She had held out a bookmark with my initials monogrammed on it and a quote that had said, "It is not what you look at, that matters, but what you see." I had tucked it into my bag, giving her my copy of Roots in exchange. We had promised to meet in Philadelphia, where I was going to Drexel and she to Villanova.

She had no alternative; she had said each time I asked her why she spent all her time studying. I must fly, she had said. I had laughed then; sure, I could not go to the US myself for my post-grad because my father would put himself through hell and back to raise the money. Vetri had stepped in, transferred the funds needed to help with the visa interview, and laughingly said I would always owe him.

Owe him I did. I have been paying for it all my life. That last morning of college had been the last time I had seen him and her before everything changed.

In my head, I had compartmentalized the men I saw in the hostel at night and the ones in the company of female classmates during the day. They were different beasts and I had never counted on seeing the two intersect. Spotting Rajesh and Vetri at the center of the mob that had fallen on her had traumatized me.

Once the campus security had led the men away, I had been summoned to the principal's office where I was told in no uncertain terms that if I did not "co-operate" the embassy would receive word of a suspicious transfer of funds to my bank account.

"Your future, Aditya," the balding man had said simply.

I chose my future. I walked away.

I do not know if Sandhya knew I had been a witness to her assault. She had not made it to the visa interview and the last I had heard, she had moved to Bangalore.

My world and understanding of men had changed that night. The assault on Sandhya had made me fearful of myself. It had made me wonder if deep down, I was the same as all those men that night. If the girl had not been Sandhya and if I had joined the group earlier for drinks, would I have been one of the feral pack of men plundering what they thought of as game?

I snap out of my reverie when I hear the screech of the microphone. I sit up and tried to focus on what is being said. My watch shows 11:00 am. I am the next presenter. I pull up the flash cards even though I could present in my sleep.

Looking around and noticing everyone engrossed, I slip out for a glass of water. Nearing the exit, I sense her before I see her. Head bent, she is poring over her presentation. I quickly slip past her and make my way out.

My phone buzzes with another message. It is Uma. Scanning the messages, I feel weary. But I resist the temptation to ignore her and text back. Turning the phone off, I head back inside. My eyes meet Sandhya's and we gaze at each other a second longer than necessary.

Instead of heading back to my table, I walk up near the stage and lean against the wall.

———

SANDHYA: THE BREAKING OF THE SPIRIT

I enter the room for the next presenter and see him there, the man from the train. I close my laptop and pick up the agenda in front of me. 'A Merging of Cultures - Aditya Raghavan' reads the entry. Aditya Raghavan. R. Aditya. It is him.

I look around. I feel hemmed in. Beads of sweat form along the base of my hairline. I feel warm enough to remove my cardigan. I get up from my seat and sit back again. I reach for the bottle of water on the table and gulp half the bottle. Inhale. Exhale. Inhale. Exhale. I close my eyes and tell myself I can get through this. I feel my heart beat return to normal. I open my eyes and look for the nearest exit should I need to make a run for it.

People are returning from breaks and he is yet to start speaking. I see him scan the room and briefly consider taking a break myself. Then I lean back and look at him. Really look at him. The years have filled him out. He is tall. Looks distinguished even. His face looks mellow, once sharp angles morphed into curves. His Adam's apple bobs as he clears his throat. His eyes are sharp. They rove around the room until they rest on me. I look away. The next time I look up, he is talking to the crowd.

His sonorous voice booms over the excellent acoustic system. It washes over me, bringing with it nostalgia and a strange kind of curiosity. I gather my belongings and whisper to my colleague that I need to step out. He gives me a raised eyebrow and nods his head. I walk quickly, hoping I am not drawing attention to myself, and hurry to the coffee shop in the lobby. There is no one there and I order a latte and grab a couple of napkins as I head to the counter for the creamer and sugar. All these years out of India have not taken the love of milk and sugar with my coffee out of me. My hands tremble as I lift the cup the barista hands to me. I find a secluded table and put my bag and laptop away.

Cupping the coffee with both hands, I look out the window. People walk with the briskness that indicates they have places to be and things to do. I look past them and my eyes fixate on the space above the shops across the street. Aditya Raghavan. A bitter feeling rises from the pit of my stomach. I remember the last time I saw him, walking away from me at the college canteen, his backpack bobbing up and down. We have promises to keep, I had told myself. Then I had been assaulted. I had gone back to the stadium to find the book I had left behind when we had left. Roots. The only gift I had ever had from him. I had heard the catcalls and the whistles. I had picked up the book and would have run if Rajesh had not stuck his foot out and tripped me.

For hours after I had come to at the hospital, I'd been incoherent. I had had no memory of what had happened. The doctor and the nurses had kept telling me that I had not been raped. Vennila had done nothing but look at me and cry. Surya had come before I was discharged, his arm bandaged. He had been mute, his eyes shrouded in pain. . I had demanded and gotten a copy of my medical records. There on paper it lay, a description of my injuries. The gash on my shoulder, the scratches on my bosom and torso, the cut on my thigh, the blow to the back of my head. There had been nothing about penetration or the possibility of pregnancy. I had felt violated, but I had had no memory of what had happened. Who had ripped my clothes? Whose hands had gone where? I had felt dirty. I had felt unclean. My parents had arrived the next morning. We had marched to the principal's office and demanded action.

"*Nothing happened. No sexual assault. She fell. It was an accident.*"

The principal had sat there, twirling the glass paper weight and not daring to look at me. I had pleaded with my parents to go to the police. Mom had backed out.

"Ille (no), Sandhya. Nothing will change. They will drag your name through the mud. They wield power. You have your future to consider. The physical wounds will heal. We will get a therapist who can help you work through your mental wounds."

My father had stayed mute. I remember feeling disgusted by his inaction. I had later wondered if he had felt powerless; if he had retreated into silence for the lack of words to make me understand that this was the fate of women everywhere.

Surya had been the first of my friends I had walked away from. He had refused to explain what had happened to me, or where he had been after I'd been admitted to hospital. The cast on his hand had looked ominous, portending secrets I had no access to. After I had threatened him with tears, he had explained to me why filing a complaint would be no good. "Your name will be spoilt. They will make sure you cannot have a proper life after this. I cannot let you ruin your life. Can't you see? No one will be willing to marry you," he had said, looking at me with all too kind eyes.

I remembered all those years when he would refuse to let me ride his bike with him. The excessive care he had taken to ensure he would not be seen alone with me around town. What had charmed me then disgusted me eventually. Later, when I had called him from Madras to find out how the bookmark, I had given Aditya had been in my bag, he had not answered my question. He had hung up instead.

In the end, I had given up. Given in. The assault had marked the end of my innocence. It had also marked the beginning of the construction of walls around my heart. The years that had followed had been tumultuous. I had run away from home, unable to share with my parents the horrors that haunted me at night. A job in Bangalore had ensured my family was at visiting distance, but emotionally out of the way. I had swapped my guarded, trusting self for someone I no longer recognized. I had been the joker and in time my mask had become me.

At work in Bangalore, I had always shown up early and stayed until the last person was gone. I had made sure I was at happy hours and every company outing. I had volunteered to organize employee events. I had made myself known. Much before there was a term for it, I had networked my way to a place way above my peers.

I hear the lobby fill up and realize with a start that Aditya's presentation must be over. Fearful of running into him, I pack up and make my way to the offices above, leaving my belongings in a pod. I then grab the lunch I packed and find a spot at some distance from the tables on the patio.

I watch my colleagues look for me before they settle to eat. Satisfied that Aditya is not here, I finish my sandwich and head back inside. I pull up my presentation one last time. Everything looks good, so I pack up and leave, promising myself I will not give him the satisfaction of knowing what he has put me through.

I must not react, I tell myself.

I check out and run smack into him.

———

ADITYA:
OF DAY DREAMS AND PEEKS INTO THE PAST

She looks at me with shock written large in her eyes. We fly apart as if by instinct and let the silence fill the distance between us. Just when it starts feeling awkward, I break it.

"Sandhya! Or is it Sandy now," I ask.

"Sandhya to old friends," she says with a wink. I am not sure what to make of this light-hearted welcome. We shake hands and realize that we are blocking the entrance. We move away.

"Join me for lunch?" I ask on an impulse.

She hesitates just a moment as if deciding how to respond. "Nah! I just ate. Also, there are things I need to get to before my presentation," she says as she leaves. I step aside and watch as she walks jauntily along the sidewalk and crosses the road. I cannot seem to move. I try to read into her demeanor and draw a blank.

I swear to myself and head to the reception desk to ask for Mr. Smith. As I wait, I watch people stream in from the conference hall. The cafe, separated from the lobby by glass walls, seems full. As I wonder if I should head out to grab lunch elsewhere, Tom shows up and hauls me inside.

Lunch passes quickly, punctuated by shop talk and subtle jabs for information. I evade pointed questions and try and fill in blanks where possible. I can feel the headache from the morning coming on when Tom indicates the beverage station. Thanking him, I pour myself a cup of hot coffee and sit back, looking at the agenda. There are two presentations before Sandhya's. Both have to do with systems I have worked with. So I decide to spend the next couple of hours in my makeshift office before returning for hers.

Tom sets me up with a temporary workspace before he leaves. I look around, impressed. They have been wooing me to shift base and move here. I currently handle the Midwest and Southern regions of the bank. Moving here will expand my portfolio and add value to my resume. I have been dithering because of Uma. I have not spoken to her about it but when Anand brought it up in the morning, I realized how much I would like to live here amid my old haunts. Having family nearby seems to make things more attractive.

In Austin, with Uma around, I walk with guilt attached to me. I hate myself for the way I treat her. Yet I resent her intrusion into my carefully ordered existence. The way she has insinuated herself into my bedroom and kitchen. The tiny bottles that line her part of the vanity, the lavender towels, the floral scents. The smell of cooking that lingers in the hallway, snaking upstairs to the bedroom and inside my closet. Sometimes I feel caught, ensnared. I feel a malaise settle on me and the beginnings of a migraine.

I call Uma. She picks up the phone, pleasantly surprised and seemingly over her displeasure with me.

"How was your morning? Did you have lunch?" I ask

"Rashmi forced me to sit with her as she worked. She has been giving me company. We just finished a nice hot lunch of rasam and vendekkai," she says. We chat briefly and I hang up.

I feel a sliver of happiness run through me. It is good to know she is getting along well with people who mean much to me.

The headache is a full-blown migraine now. I wince at the bright light streaming through the window. I draw the blinds and dig out my trusty box of Excedrin. Swallowing a dose, I set an alarm on my phone, lay my head against the cool surface of the desk and close my eyes. A series of images form, merge, and dance around my head. I am not sure if I am awake or asleep. I try to open my eyes but the medication-induced haze and the chill of the desk is compelling.

#

I am at school, a transplant from elitist Delhi. My competency in English, legendary at my old school, marks me here as a joke. I struggle with being bullied. The other boys make fun of my accent. I take to heading to the library during recess and lunch break. Almost always, I find Sandhya there. After she leaves, I pick up the book she has been reading and force myself to read it. Over time, I grow to enjoy the books. She seems to favor the classics. I veer towards non-fiction. I check out books by Stephen Covey.

#

I do not know how it happened, but I have changed. The boys who once made fun of me now want to surround me. I like this power. I also realize this power is tenuous. I have learned the rules of the game now. I do not ever mention Sandhya in conversation, knowing she will be picked on if I do.

#

I am in college, sticking close to Vetri. Being close to the nerve center affords me invincibility as well as invisibility. In some sense, I no longer exist. I seem to be only the sum of what I imbibe from my surroundings.

#

I am rediscovering myself. In the snatches of time I get to spend with Sandhya, I understand what it is like to be understood without speaking a word, to be felt without a touch, to be in love without expressing it.

#

I am on the phone. Surya is demanding that I call Vetri and ask him to meet me at the old bus stop. He tells me that I am not to go. Remember to be seen with your friends, he exhorts. I feel both fear and fearlessness. I remember the past hour in the principal's office. I call Vetri without hesitation.

#

My visa is through. I sort through the bags I brought back with me from the hostel. There is absolutely nothing I want to take with me to my new world. I wonder where I left the bookmark.

#

I am headed to America. I am confident in myself. I watch and I learn. Everybody likes to orbit a leader. The games people play have less to do with ability and more to do with their aptitude to morph and change. I do not recognize myself anymore. Without Sandhya to moor me, I am adrift.

Someone is shaking me. Tom is by my shoulder, gently shaking me awake. I open my eyes and hope I have not been drooling. I cannot seem to make sense of my disjointed dream. I gather my things and make a detour to the restroom to splash water on my face.

My phone indicates that Sandhya's presentation must have started. We walk in as she is pointing something out on the screen and explaining how the logic is implemented in their software. I find a table and focus. Her voice is crisp, rising and falling as she explains what she means. I am taken by the minimalist slides, the use of just black and gray. I scribble notes on my copy of her presentation and jot down questions for later.

There are also other questions in my head. What happened after she had left the college grounds in a cacophony of siren sounds and blinking lights? How did she deal with the trauma of what had happened? Had she heard about what happened to Vetri and Rajesh? Is she married? What was her job? How did she end up in Philadelphia where she (we) would have been if she had gone to Villanova?

I involuntarily glance up and check her left hand. The solid gold on her ring finger gives off a dull shine. I look at her face, scouring it. For what? Happiness? Pain? I am not sure.

She is done and the next presenter takes her place. I look around and catch her looking at me. I nod and she acknowledges me. I know I must talk to her and soon. I suppose I could walk away this time too. But will I? Should I?

———

SANDHYA:
OF SPOUSES WHO HAVE YOUR BACK

I am doing the dishes as Vikram walks in. He seems run down and tired. "Long day?" I ask. "Just a regular day with more than its share of emergencies," he says and yawns. He smells of mulch and cattle. "Run along and take a shower. I will set the table for dinner," I say. He looks at me gratefully before he ascends the steps to our master suite. I turn my attention to the dishes and suddenly feel comforted by the solid, stable presence of him.

I am setting the dishes on the table as he comes down, smelling of tea tree oil and musk. His hair is wet and the locks curl at the base of his neck. He pulls out a chair and uncovers each dish, sniffing appreciatively. We eat in companionable silence.

"I met Aditya today," I say. He looks at me strangely.

"Someone from college?"

"How do you know?" I ask.

"The last time you had a nightmare, you called out to him."

I am puzzled. "Why would I do that?" I ask

Vikram looks at me sadly. "I do not know, Sandhu. Usually, when you have a nightmare, you flail your arms and legs as if you are fighting. You open your mouth, but no sound comes out. Eventually you find your voice and then the scream is unnatural." He flinches as he says that.

"You rock back and forth while I hold you. At that point you usually realize that it is me holding you. But this last time, you kept calling for an Aditya and I did not know who this person was. I attributed it to the news articles you had been reading. Perhaps that is triggering something in your memory? Do you think Aditya was part of the group who attacked you?"

I shake my head, distinctly remembering Rajesh tripping me and seeing Vetri. The other guys had been strangers. I had not seen Aditya with them.

"No, Aditya was not part of the group. At least I do not remember seeing him. Months later, back in Madras, when I was sorting through my college stuff before I left for Bangalore, I found this bookmark I had gifted Aditya on the last day of college. We had shared a love of books and I had felt I had to mark our friendship with something. So I had this bookmark engraved with a quote and his initials. I still have it with me. I do not know why I cannot bring myself to throw it out."

I pause and Vikram nods, encouraging me to go on. "I had no idea how I had come by it. I asked Surya and Vennila and they would not tell me anything. I tried finding Aditya's contacts through mutual friends and it was like he had disappeared. This was before email, Google, and Facebook. There was no way for me to reach him. I could not help wondering if he had had something to do with it all. It is like he holds a missing piece of the puzzle and I need that to feel whole again."

I pause again. "God! I am talking like my therapist now," I say lightly and continue.

"Well, I saw him on the train this morning but was not sure it was him. Then I realized that he is part of the management team that is visiting from Austin. He presented before lunch. I could not sit through the presentation and so I left. When I came back after lunch, I ran into him like, literally.

"I do not know, Vik. I feel so conflicted. He had been my friend. At least I think he had been. I even think he may have had feelings for me before the end of college. We were to come to Philadelphia together. He was headed to Drexel and I to Villanova. Then everything changed. Today, seeing him brought back so much of the past."

I am crying at this point. I let the tears flow.

"He asked me to go to lunch with him but I ran away. He is probably in town until tomorrow. I know I must talk to him at some point. I just did not have the energy or the courage to do it today."

I wipe my eyes with a napkin and try to pull myself together.

"I did some asking around and it looks like he might be taking over our region," I tell Vikram. "I'm not sure how I feel about it. For years, I went around not knowing if he knew something I did not. Seeing him today brought all of it back. I feel ripped and raw."

I wipe my eyes again and put a spoonful of chhole in my mouth to stop Vikram from coming around the table to comfort me. I suddenly feel a deep need to walk away and shut myself up in a place where no one can reach me. To curl into a ball and wait until all this passes away.

Vikram chews his food slowly and takes a deep breath before he starts to talk.

"I do not know what happened, but if you feel Aditya has answers you need, perhaps you should talk to him. Who knows what made him walk away then? We all change, Sandhu. The person you were then and the person you are now are different. I am sure he has changed too."

My appetite is gone and I push my plate away. "Maybe things have changed, but I feel hurt, Vik. I do not want to bring it all up and rehash it. To what point? Is it going to give me back all those nights I wake up screaming and shivering? Is it going to give me back the ability to relax if I am alone in the dark? I have lost so much, Vik. I am unable to trust. I am unable to relax enough to enjoy lovemaking. So much of my life would have been different if it were not for the blank space I have in my head. Did you know that after I woke up and spoke to the people around me, their first concern was for my reputation?"

I laugh hysterically.

"They wanted to know what use it would be for me to find out what had happened. One of them said that by pursuing action, I would be spoiling my future as well as those of the guys who attacked me. What I went through was not even an afterthought, Vik. No one cared, least of all the people I thought were friends. They would not even tell me who had assaulted me. If I had not seen the bookmark later, I would have had no clue that Aditya had even been involved. There was a time, Vik, when I considered him a friend. We had been at school together before college. Later in college, we had worked on our grad school applications together. We had traded books. We had had something, a relationship based on our love for books. There had been a time when I had wondered if, when we studied together in the US, we may have something that went past friendship."

My voice seems to have sunk to a whisper. I realize I am talking as much to myself as I am talking to him. We both rise and clear the table. As I pack away the leftovers, he works silently by my side. When we are done, he gathers me to him and we walk to the love seat where I lean on him. The silence seems oppressive.

"Let's watch TV," I say.

"Do you want to talk?" he says.

I shake my head and switch the TV on. We stretch our legs out and pretend to watch a show.

I play over our interactions from the day. Did I see anything akin to apology in Aditya's face? I am not sure. It just seemed as though he was keen to reconnect. There was none of the awkwardness one would expect at running into someone you do not want to meet. Perhaps I should do what he is doing and pretend we have no history. Nothing will change, right? He will go back to his life and I to mine. Except for the what-ifs haunting me.

Just coming to a decision seems to lift a weight off my being. I seek out Vikram's palm, only to realize he is already asleep. I prod him gently and we walk upstairs. He seeks his side of the bed and I mine, His snores fill the room while I toss and turn. I wanted to be in his arms today, to be held and loved, to feel safe. But he is asleep.

I feel resentment now. For everything that had happened in the past. For the trauma that has robbed lovemaking of its charm. I am tempted to wake Vikram and cuddle into his arms. Instead, I lie wide awake and ponder the questions I would ask Aditya if I did decide to meet with him.

Sleep still eluding me, I pull up my laptop and hop from blog to blog, catching up on my virtual friends. They offer me solace that no living being can. Pulled into the vortex of their problems, I forget mine. I live vicariously through those who battle infertility and go on to have babies. I walk along with people experiencing issues in their married life and reassure them that all will be well. In the grand void of anonymity online, I read The Sun Goddess's blog.

Mistake?

What if someday you wake up and realize you have been living a lie? Sometimes I feel that way. I have spent the better part of my 20s chasing dreams. Dreams of Mister. Now that I am his wife, I am not sure what I saw in him. The Mister who faded in and out of my life in snatches had this brooding part to him. Something I attributed to his charm. Up close and personal, all that brooding is getting stale. I am tired of the games. Sometimes I want to rip the mask off and call it quits.

Night night!

The Sun Goddess

I feel a sadness descend on me. I type up a comment and then discard it. Sleep claims me with offerings of disturbing dreams.

ADITYA: OF WALKS AND LIFE'S MUSINGS

I stroll along 15th and Market, merging into the crowd of people wrapping scarves around their necks and throwing their jackets on as they exit walled-off glass offices and hurry home. I detour and find myself at the Reading Terminal. I check my pocket by force of habit to check that my phone is there. I realize that I had switched it off before my presentation and had not turned it back on. I let it be. I need this time to clear my head and figure out what I want out of my life.

I wander among the throngs of people buying dinner. The smell of fish mixes with that of day-old plastic wrapped flowers and assaults my nostrils. I tug my jacket closer and wade deeper till I find a cozy cafe. Buying a biscotti and coffee, glad I had checked in and left my bag at the hotel, I sit and watch people pass by. I notice a girl perhaps a few years older than Vibha sitting by herself, lost in a book amid all this noise. I notice a family ambling along with a child in a stroller. Goldfish crackers rattle in the tray as the child grabs a handful. I smile wistfully. I notice the man has his arm firmly against his woman's back, guiding her as much as claiming possession. I wish I had brought a book along.

My thoughts turn to Uma. Our marriage is an unqualified disaster, says a voice in my head. Being away from home should not feel like relief. But it does. Now that I have admitted it to myself, I feel the weight ease off my mind. I think of Uma. Pretty, eager to please. I think of myself

Cynical. I feel tension build at the base of my neck. I am clenching my jaws. This is yet another mess I can blame on only myself. I seem to be drawn to situations I have little to do with, but with all the responsibility. I wonder what I am going to tell Uma. I think of facing my parents, her parents, our siblings, and my heart sinks. What do I say? That I made a mistake? That I am not cut out for marriage? That I am too set in my ways to change? That Uma and I are not compatible?

I can hear the recriminations in my head, the tears, and the emotional blackmail inherent in these situations. For a minute anger creeps up on me. Can Uma not see we are blatantly incompatible? Why does she act the martyr all the time? Why does she give me her all? I feel petulant. If she had asked for a divorce and called me names, how much easier would this be? I drain my coffee and leave the warmth of the cafe for the cold outside.

I look back to our wedding night. Uma, coy in her bridal sari. Eyes bright, face flushed, waiting for me. All I had wanted to do was sleep. The let-down on her face as she had changed into her night clothes and withdrawn beneath the covers had shamed me. We had kept busy enough to have little time to ourselves over the next few days. The good-natured ribbing and the company of the people who loved us had kept me from dwelling on the lack of emotion I felt towards her. I had attributed it to being part of an arranged marriage. I'd been sure that once left to our own devices, we would figure it out.

On the flight home, stuck beside each other for over twenty hours, we had talked. She had spoken about her childhood (cloyingly sweet), relationships with her siblings (very amiable), cousins (close friends), school, college, work (variations of a big party all the time), shopping (punctuated by brands). I had listened with as much interest as I could muster. Perhaps I had been judgmental, but I replayed the conversation in my head and could not find a single thing to connect with. As I had shared snippets of my life with her, talking about the books I had enjoyed, her eyes had glazed over. By the time I had started talking about my work, she had nodded off. To my credit, I had been awake the entire time during her conversation.

Back home, everything she did seemed to draw my ire. I did not want to be looked after. "I do not need a mother." I had yelled one morning after she woken up yet another day at 5:00 am, packed my lunch and made a hot breakfast. All I had wanted was for her to be herself. I had wanted her to show some interest in her surroundings. To talk about what she wanted to do with her life. She had seemed to have enjoyed her work in Bangalore, but any mention of going back to school or working now seemed to be of no interest to her.

I had felt trapped in a bizarre nightmare of my own making. The only times I had ever seen her animated was when we visited her cousins. She would disappear in the kitchen with Devika and I would hear giggles. Conversation around the dinner table would include discussions of the latest Indian soaps, movies, design trends. Her smile would reach her eyes and her face would be flushed with genuine happiness. The glow would last all the ride home and then we would withdraw to our secluded worlds. The difference in our ages had stood out starkly after each of these visits.

Any attempts at conversation had gone nowhere. We shared no common interests. I loved reading and books. She loved Bollywood and celeb magazines. I preferred a quiet weekend at home, waking late, cooking an elaborate meal, and watching a movie on Netflix. She preferred eating out and a movie at the theaters. I loved black and gray and she was as vibrant as a rainbow. Her energy sapped me.

I pull out my phone and power it on. I see three missed calls and voice messages from Uma. My text messages show a red 10 next to it. I sigh and play the last message.

"I am worried Aditya. Please call."

I call her and she answers at the first ring. She seems to be smiling as she answers the phone.

"Are you alright? I saw all your missed calls and messages only now. I had powered my phone off before my presentation and forgot to turn it on," I try to explain.

"Why would I not be? I only wanted to make sure you were okay" she says. "Rashmi and Anand are so much fun to be with. They all liked the gifts I got for them. Vibha was thrilled with all the color coordinated accessories I got for her."

"What did you get for Anand and Rashmi?" I ask, curiosity getting the better of me.

"NFL gear for Anand and bake ware for Rashmi." She answers easily. I feel uneasy about the thoughts that had been in my head a little while ago. I am conciliatory as I prepare to hang up.

"Sleep tight. I will try and wrap up early and get home tomorrow."

"Night night!" she replies and laughs at something Rashmi or Vibha says in the background.

I put the laptop away and brush my teeth before I settle on the bed and pick up Groff's Arcadia. With the day behind me, I should have been able to get caught up in it, but Sandhya worms herself into my head and I put the book away. I grab the laptop and look her up on the company intranet. Soon I follow a trail online that leads me to her LinkedIn. I look up people we have in common and realize Anand and Sandhya are connected. Interesting , I think, and pull up her Facebook profile. It is sparse and I cannot see her pictures or her friends list. I type her name in on Google and in a matter of minutes land on her book review blog. I smile and dig into the archives.

———

UMA: OF NIGHTLY STROLLS
AND HELPFUL STRANGERS

I hang up the phone and look wistfully at Vibha who is walking ahead with Anand. I am reminded of that time my period was late and how panicked I felt. Devika had taken me to the Ob/Gyn who had confirmed I was not pregnant. I had gotten a prescription for birth control pills then and continued to use them ever since.

I had been sure I did not want to bring a child into this world if Aditya and I could not figure out how to make our marriage work. Seeing Vibha and the easy relationship she shares with her parents makes me want to talk to Aditya, to force a decision. The journal has been weighing on me as well. I see two sides to Aditya. The rare concern that seems genuine and an apathy that seems to stem from some underlying discontent. I have a feeling Sandhya holds the key to my happiness.

I am tempted to ask Rashmi if she knows Sandhya. Anand and Aditya go back a long way. If he knew, chances are Rashmi would too. I walk, lost in thought, trying to find an opening when Anand speaks up.

"Uma, you seem quiet. Did Aditya say anything to upset you?" I shake my head and walk faster to catch up with them.

"You lived in Coimbatore, right, when Aditya was at college?" I ask. Anand nods. "We are as thick as thieves," he says and laughs jovially. "Do you know all his friends?" I ask. He sobers up. "Why do you ask?" I give in and take him into confidence.

"Aditya and I know each other only because our families are friends. I am realizing these days that I hardly know him. I mean, I know what he likes to eat and the kind of clothes he likes to wear and the everyday living stuff. But other things—like his friends from school and college, any crushes he had had—that kind of stuff we have never talked about," I say and let Anand process my words.

"You should ask him," he says after a few minutes. I nod and walk along silently. Anand speaks again. "Aditya is a loner mostly. He had a good set of friends at college in Coimbatore. Then the last day of college there was some kind of incident and he changed." He pauses as if wondering if he had given away too much.

On a hunch I ask, "Does it involve Sandhya?"

Anand relaxes, thinking I know about Sandhya. I hold my breath and hope he will continue.

"Sandhya was his classmate from school. He liked her, really liked her." He looks at me significantly. I catch his meaning and nod. "Well, on the last day, a few guys roughed her up and Aditya found her. They were supposed to have gone to do their Masters together, but she never showed up for the visa interview. I do not think they have talked since. The last I asked him, he said he had heard through the grapevine that she was working in Bangalore."

I let out the air I have been holding.

"That's sad," I say. "If they were friends, they should have stayed in touch, right?" I notice with relief that we are approaching the house. I change tacks and ask Anand, "How many people are you expecting for your holiday party this Saturday?"

He looks at me shrewdly before he answers. "About sixty people. We are catering the food. Should be a good mix of people." Rashmi joins us and we all walk inside together.

"Do you have pictures of you all growing up?" I ask. My question seems to cheer Anand and Rashmi and they enthusiastically pull out old albums. We sit late into the night, poring over old pictures and talking about everyone in the family.

I see bits and pieces of the boy that had been in the Aditya I know. I remember some good bits. Chancing on him one evening as he sat on the terrace of his house, writing in a journal. He had pushed it out of view when he had seen me. There had been another occasion as I had walked home from school, when I had seen him trying a smoke at the corner shop with some friends. "He does not belong," is I had thought then. Perhaps he has never belonged anywhere, I think now.

For a moment, hope fills my heart. I go to bed feeling that maybe I will figure this puzzle out.

<hr />

Coal or diamond?

Today, I got a chance to look through old pictures of the Mister. There was one of him sitting on the terrace of his house, a book in hand, lost to the world. There was a vulnerability to him that had me wanting to reach out and stroke his cheek.

I wonder if there are parts of ourselves we never show the world. Parts we keep safe, hidden, not to be shared with anyone.

If Mister had known he was being photographed, what would the picture have looked like? Would he have struck a pose? Would he have pretended to not notice? Would there have been artifice? Insolence maybe? Or would he have been guarded?

It made me think of the games we play. The masks we wear. I have been wearing one for five years now. I have pretended to myself that all is well, that things will change, that the masks will come off and we will show our honest selves to each other.

Today, I held a mirror up to myself and asked hard questions. What am I waiting for? How much do I want this relationship to work? Where do I want to go from here? How much more can I take?

While I do not have the answers, I feel relief just being able to voice the thoughts in my head. I know I am rambling but there is too much happening in my head and I cannot put it down in words.

So today I am making myself a promise. I am going to let go of the pretenses. I am going to look at this relationship without the baggage of past expectations. And most importantly, I am going to be honest with the Mister.

Today's song recommendation: Someone like you - Adele

Ciao!

The Sun Goddess

SANDHYA: OF FRIENDSHIPS GONE SOUR

"It's Friday!" I say aloud and slide off the bed. Vikram squints and assesses me before burrowing back under the blankets. He covers his head with the pillow for good measure.

"Wake up, you lazy bum!" I prod him with my finger. He shoos me away and turns to his side. I give up and waltz into the bathroom. I sit on the toilet and realize I have my period. The happiness from a few minutes ago evaporates. Every month I tell myself I will be an adult about it, but watching the blood spread in the water, tendrils of red staining and discoloring the clear surface, reminds me of how broken I am. I reach for a tampon and rue my life.

The first few years had slipped past unnoticed. Then the years of actively trying had filled me with hope. Each day I took my temperature, recording it dutifully, charting the rise and fall and reveling in my ability to predict ovulation and bleeding. Then, as each month passed, I waited, poking my breasts for telltale tautness and pain. As my temperature dropped, so did my spirits. I soldiered on gamely, telling myself, it takes only one. Months became years and despondency set in. The hope that had once blazed strong died down to embers.

Then a stray thought had niggled its way into my head, embedding itself there securely. What if the assault caused my infertility? What if they had damaged me so badly that I could never bear children? I had been examined all right, and told it had not been rape, but why hadn't I checked with other doctors for a second opinion?

Talking to Amma had not helped. She had kept repeating that I was okay, as if by telling me that, all would be fine. Sometimes, I wished I could be like her and pretend all was well.

I marched, Vikram by my side, to the first OB/GYN I could find near home and walked out with a laundry list of tests. "Were you prescribed any medication after your assault?" the kind doctor had asked after I had recounted blandly what had happened to me. I had looked at her blankly, having no idea.

"Does it matter?" I had asked

"It may," she said.

I had dutifully had my blood drawn, my vagina forced open by a cold speculum, had dye injected inside my uterus and so on till the nightmares had started featuring doctors as well.

———

As the months passed, I had haunted forums online, poured my frustrations out to Rashmi and bonded with her over IVF protocols.

"What is your diagnosis?" she had asked, familiar with the med-speak in the way that only someone who has walked the walk can be.

"Unexplained," I had said, knowing that single word had included not just my fertility diagnosis.

After the two rounds of IVF my insurance would cover, I had given up, opting to term myself childfree instead of childless.

But the hope had never died. Somewhere inside of me, I ached to see Vikram's eyes and my smile come together in a baby. Each period was a visual reminder of what could not be.

I clean myself and step to the vanity to brush my teeth. My phone pings, signaling incoming email. Relieved for something to take my mind off the dark thoughts in my head, I reach out for the phone.

"Sandhya, people are looking at your LinkedIn profile," says an email. Curious, I open the app and see Aditya's name under 'Who's viewed you.' The euphoria of the morning gives way to reality. I put the phone away and think of what I want to do. The conference ends today and he likely will be flying out tonight. I suspect he is with the head office in Austin. I may end up having to work with him.

I turn over this possibility in my head. I am certain he knows something I do not. His bookmark is in my bag after all. Pretending nothing had happened is not going to do me any good. I decide to have it out and feel better at having decided. I also make up my mind to be civil. More importantly, I will ask him all the questions burning a hole in my head. I have been brutally direct all my life.

In the initial years after college, he had often been in my thoughts, the orange tasseled bookmark a constant reminder of how things had gone that day. I had considered throwing it away but held on to it as a way to remember all that had happened. My therapist had been curious about it. She figured it was my way of accepting that something had happened and that I needed closure. It is still stuck in my bag somewhere. I had not read the book he'd given me either. Just like that book mark, it was linked to that fateful day.

They say time heals. I am not sure. It just creates a distance from the event and gives you perspective. I have accepted that what had happened had not been my mistake. It had been incidental. I had been in the wrong place at the wrong time.

The question of 'why me?' however, still haunts me. It is infrequent now, I must admit. I have moved on in some sense. I rarely think of my attackers. In the first few years, I had burned with a powerless rage to think they could do this to me and go on and live their lives as though nothing had happened. I had considered keeping tabs on them to see how their lives had turned out. Curiously, it was Usha who had deterred me.

"You cannot change what has happened, Sandhu, you can only choose how you react. By living in the past, you are letting go of your future," she had told me. I would have dismissed her preachy advice but it had resonated with me. I had thought it over and let it go symbolically, releasing a couple of balloons in Cubbon Park one day to take with them my rage and hunger for bad things to befall my attackers. I did not think I could forgive them but I could attempt to forget.

My mind goes back to the LinkedIn email. If Aditya had been looking at me online, I should probably find out what he has been up to myself, I think.

I rush through the morning and settle into my compartment on the train. With an hour to kill, I pull up his name on Google. Beyond the LinkedIn profile, little shows up. I click on the images tab and stumble on to an album by ARagz. I scan the pictures, trying to find out it if it is him. Finding nothing personal, I pull up LinkedIn again and trawl through his connections list.

Anand.

He is connected to Anand. The cousin from Peelamedu he had said he hung out with over the weekends. That Anand was this Anand? I rack my brains, trying to remember where Anand had said he had gone to college and where he had been from. All our conversations had been casual. Any identity Anand had in my head was only that of Rashmi's husband.

It seems like all the webs around me are connected. I close my eyes and think of Rashmi. Laughing, goofy Rashmi. The girl who had dragged me to her home most afternoons for chai and gupshup as she called it. We had spent many an afternoon roaming around the King of Prussia mall, stopping before store windows, gaping, and giggling. She had tried to teach me how to wear makeup. I had given up after taking one look at myself in the mirror. I hate artifice and that seems to apply to all parts of my life.

I look back on our time together and a sadness fills me when I think of what I call the beginning of the end. That fateful day she had announced her pregnancy while I had miscarried. I had been happy for her. How could I not have been? Yet, my heart had felt like it could burst with envy. I coveted what she had. Perhaps it was self-preservation, but I had shut down, withdrawn into a shell. I had heard of Vibha's birth over email and visited only when she was three months old. Lingering just enough for some tea for old times' sakes. We stood at the door, unable to bridge the gap, and I left.

When we had run into each other at the homes of mutual friends, we had steered clear of the one topic that had bound us and fill our interactions with everything that did not matter. Until she had called early this week, I had forgotten all about her. She had said her home was in Wayne.

A light bulb goes on in my head. Aditya had boarded the train at Wayne. Is he staying with them? As if on cue, Wayne approaches and I brace myself to see him standing there. I feel a mixture of relief and disappointment when I do not spot him.

I continue browsing and end up with few clues about him. Facebook gives me one hit that looks like him. But I can see nothing of his profile. If he is on there, he is well hidden.

I put the phone away and pull out my laptop to get started on my emails. I am lost in them when a new mail notification pops up. "Lunch?" asks the subject. I click on it to find a short note from Aditya.

————

Sandhya,

I am leaving this Sunday and would like to catch up before that. Will you have lunch with me today?

Aditya

————

I read the email a couple of times. Terse. Crisp. No traces of anything personal.

I compose a few different replies before I settle on one that mimics his.

Aditya,

I can do lunch. Meet you around noon at the lobby.

Sandhya

———

I find it hard to focus on work so I close my work email and decide to surf instead. I blog hop and land on The Sun Goddess. Mentally sending good vibes her way, I pull up an old post of hers. A favorite of mine. The one she had written when she got inked. A beautiful butterfly on her left shoulder. But then, in this weather, who was going to run around wearing sleeveless clothes?

Realizing the next stop will be Suburban Station, I close all windows and log off. I make my way to the office before the day's presentations and find a pod where I can leave my bag. I find a clutch of colleagues in the cafeteria and join them. They seem nervous and on edge. I stay in the periphery, listening to their conversations.

I gather that they are all curious about the direction the company will take after the merger. The sales and marketing teams are sure they will be let go. Their talk is about severance and who is hiring in the area. The tech guys seem sure that they have nothing to worry about. If anything, hiring should see an uptick with upgrades and new development in the works, they feel.

I feel insulated from all of this. I should be concerned, but I am not. The run-in with Aditya has shifted my world off balance, skewing perspectives, and re-centering priorities. I am tempted to look back on the past, to dissect all the paths not taken and wonder about alternate universes.

I look at the time and decide to head to the conference over at the next building. I am not presenting and the only slot that is of any interest is the CIO presentation which is the first for the day. I grab my purse, lock the cabinet that holds my laptop bag, and rush outside. It is decidedly cold for this time of the year. I thrust my fingers into my jacket and raise the hood to cover my neck, walking with my head down.

I find a seat towards the exit and settle down. Familiar faces smile as they head towards their cliques. My team converges on me and soon the air is abuzz with Friday evening plans. "Want to join us for lunch?" Sam asks and I shake my head. "Have plans," I say and smile. Talk turns to Vikram and detours to Sam's Labrador, Ella. We are interrupted by the sounds of the program starting and a hush falls on the room.

———

ADITYA: REMINISCENCES

I fell asleep last night with the laptop open. Somewhere around midnight, I woke with a jerk and put everything away before sliding under the covers. Now, sleep eludes me. My thoughts keep going back to my last conversation with Uma. Maybe because this is the first time that we are with people who have known me for years, but my actions seem strange even to me. I try to imagine Anand accepting an offer without telling Rashmi and it horrifies me. Is this who I am?

Watching Anand and Rashmi and the ease with which they work with each other has me thinking about Uma. It is as if I now see the past five years through a different lens. I am not happy with what I see. The incongruity of our isolation in Austin, the bubble we have been in, seems stark when contrasted with what I see here. It makes me wonder why Uma has put up with everything I have put her through.

I should have discussed the offer to move to Philly with her. Had I already decided not to accept? Having come here, I see how much more it will do for my career. In some sense, maybe moving here will be a new start for both of us? I mull over it and decide I should talk it over with her before I make a final decision.

I fall into a dreamless sleep and wake up refreshed. I call Anand's home number before I head to work and ask to speak to Uma. Anand tells me that bringing her along was the best thing I had done. She is a lovely girl and they had a good time going over old family pictures.

I feel a twinge of regret for having stayed back in the city. "We should do it again tonight with me." I say and hear Uma's voice.

"Hello! Did you sleep well?"

"Yes, I did. You?"

"We had a great time sitting up late and sharing stories of your childhood. Looks like you have a fun side to you that only I am not aware of."

Underneath her teasing voice, I register sadness. For once, I wonder if I had been wrong about her all along.

"Do you want go out to dinner with me tonight? Just the two of us?" I ask.

"How about we all go out? I am sure Rashmi could use a break from the kitchen and all of us can catch up."

I agree, feeling a tad disappointed, and hang up.

At the office, I settle in at one of the temporary work areas and log in. A note from the CIO is at the top of the list.

Aditya,

If you have time this morning, I would like to see you for about half hour before lunch. I am situated in the Elmer room for the day. Let me know if you can make it.

Tim.

I wonder what he could want to talk to me about. Other than the lunch meeting with Sandhya and a presentation later in the day, my calendar is open. I reply saying I will see him at 11:30 am.

I had started my career with the bank as an intern right out of college and then accepted the developer position they had offered me.

Databases were my specialty. I had stayed late, worked weekends, and made it to manager within the first five years. Opting for a lateral move, I had moved over to the business side and found it a natural fit. These days I have been doing a lot of research and trying to figure out where the market is headed. I head online banking now. I am trying to recruit and build a team to work on a digital payments for the bank. I love my work and the fact that my workday is flexible. With the merger, the task of navigating the other bank's systems and finding out what to keep is part of my portfolio. I can see advantages to moving out here. I wonder if that is what Tim wants to speak to me about.

I process my other emails and on impulse look Sandhya up on the intranet. If I do end up moving here, she will be part of my team. I wonder if she realizes that. I play back our latest interaction and am suddenly not sure what to expect at lunch today. I am more nervous than I want to admit. Shankar's revelation has been playing in my head. I wonder how much Sandhya thinks of the past. Obviously, it has been years and she has gotten on with her life. But how does one erase something like this from their head? I remember my nightmares and part of me aches for her.

In the days following the assault, I had shut myself in my room, only stepping out for meals. No one at home had known of what happened. It had taken place on the last day of college and in the evening. The authorities had not even had to send a message to the families of the hostel students. On the train back, my mind had played over the scene again and again. What had Rajesh and Vetri been thinking? Had they done it because it was Sandhya or had she just been in the wrong place at the wrong time? The money sitting in my bank account had weighed on me. My dad had heaved a sigh of relief when I had told him that a friend was helping with the finances. Ashwin had smirked and remarked, "friends in high places" and laughed about it. Amma had been visiting temples and breaking coconuts for Lord Ganesha so I would get my visa. So much had seemed to be riding on it.

When I had got my visa and called Vetri to let him know his money was wired back, someone at his residence had picked up the phone and agreed to pass the message on. I had been relieved I did not have to deal with him. By mid-August, my bags had been packed and the phone lines had been burning with messages from extended family near Philadelphia. Amma had been happy that Anand lived nearby.

Anand had come to pick me up at the airport. I had stayed with him for a week before moving to an apartment I was to share with three other guys. Anand and Rashmi had sent me off stocked with cooked food and ready to eat meals. The nights had been hard. I had woken up most days with a panic attack. The same jokes involving women I had heard at college repulsed me now. I was labeled weird and left behind when plans were made for Friday nights and weekends. Most weekends, I ended up staying at school. Other times, I went to Anand's home. I took on extra classes and graduated ahead of time.

Often, I wonder what would have happened if Sandhya had not gone back to the stadium. Would we have dated? Would we have married? So much of my life seems to be tied to her. I had stayed clear of marriage and women for years before I gave in. Even if I had not really spent much time thinking of her, she has been occupying my head for over a decade now. Our lunch weighs heavily on my mind.

The reminder on my laptop tells me I have 15 minutes before my meeting. I use the men's room and head to the Elmer room.

"Come in!" a quiet voice says. I step in and Tim is a tiny man behind the desk. I extend my hand and he pumps it with vigor, as if to make up for his lack of height. I take a seat.

"Thanks for coming to see me at short notice. I will get straight to the point. I am aware that Steve made you an offer to move to this region and you are thinking about it. I do think you are the right man for the position. However, there is a small wrinkle." He stops and smiles at me. "Steve is accepting a promotion, so if you accept the offer to move, you will have to take his place. I believe you are more than adequately qualified for the position." He pauses and lets it all sink in.

I am listening, my mind awash with possibilities and questions, when he continues. "If you are interested, I can set up time after you are back in Austin to talk about the specifics. I will appreciate it if you will give it consideration and get back to me by next week." He stands up, signaling the end of the conversation.

I assure him that I am honored by his consideration and that I will let him know.

Walking out, I make a mental note to talk to Uma as soon as I get home. When the offer to move had initially come, I had been sure I would decline. My guilt at having married Uma and not being compatible with her had been eating at me. At least she had family in Austin she could fall back on. Now that she has met Anand and Rashmi and seems to get along fabulously with them, perhaps moving would not be such a bad idea. A drive after dinner would be a good time to talk to her about it, I think.

———

SANDHYA: BROACHING THE PAST

I clap enthusiastically, following the cues of the people around me. Tim, our new CIO, seems to project a presence that belies his size. It is not often that management folks talk to you with conviction. If this man is any indication, the company seems to be in the right path, I think. I am excited by the prospects he has painted.

I look at the agenda as silence falls gently in the aftermath of the cheer. The rest of the day has presentations to do with accounting, legal and intellectual property. I could blow it all off without anybody noticing or caring. A voice from the podium insinuates itself into my head and I look up. The head of the division I work for is talking about the implications of the re-org on our business unit.

I should be listening, but I am jumpy. The specter of lunch with Aditya haunts me. I am caught between skipping it altogether and forcing him to talk about our past. Where would I start? What if he stonewalled and pretended nothing had happened? I feel panic rising in my body. I am fidgety.

A tug at my sleeve has me turning. The group around me is listening intently and my neighbor is pointing for me to look up and listen. I stop doodling and focus instead. My doodles have somehow morphed into stick figures, one prone on the ground and one walking away. Trees surround the two figures. The sun is breaking through. Perhaps my subconscious is trying to tell me something. As the presentation wraps up, I carefully fold the sheet of paper and tuck it into my bag. I hurry outside before my group can drag me to the cafe for coffee. I find a secluded spot near the parking entrance and dial Vikram.

"He wants to have lunch with me," I say without preamble.

"Have lunch. Do not make it a bigger deal than it is. It is just food and conversation. Walk out anytime you are not comfortable. Ask him about the book mark." Vikram is the voice of reason and I find myself nodding as I listen to him. I check my bag as if to reassure myself that the book mark is in there somewhere.

"Love you," I say out of habit.

"Love you too!" Vikram says before he hangs up.

The clock reads 10:30 am. I have an hour or more to kill before lunch. The idea of listening to legal stuff makes me sleepy, so I push open the door and walk into the early winter sunshine. I walk slowly, noticing the small details that I usually miss in my rush to get in on time. The sun feels warm and lifts my spirits. I spy a tiny used books store innovatively named 'Second Chances' and walk inside. A chime jingles to indicate they have customers. The lady at the counter moves as if to come over and help me. I shake my head to indicate I am just browsing. The shelves hold an eclectic collection of books. I spy an old copy of Roots by Alex Haley. I remember the book Aditya had given me. The one I had left behind in Madras in a token resistance to what fate had handed me. I put it in my basket. A beautifully illustrated copy of The Little Prince grabs my attention. I am lost in the smell of old books and low piped music.

I settle myself on a wicker chair by the window and thumb through The Little Prince.

"I thought you were my rose."

The thought comes unbidden in my head. I read the book with the sunlight falling on me. The door opens to let another customer in. My reverie is broken and I pull myself up with effort, pay for the books and head out again. I decide to get back to the lobby and wait there. As I walk in, I see Aditya sitting on one of the sofas, typing away on his Mac. I hesitate and before I can turn away, he looks up and smiles. Closing his laptop, he puts it aside and crosses the distance between us in long strides. His warm hand encases mine and he says, "Hello!"

I am aware of his musky scent. I am aware of his physical proximity. My reaction to him surprises me. I lean away to put some distance between us. He notices and lets go of my hand sharply. We walk to the sofa and sit wordlessly for a minute while he packs his bag.

I am taking in everything I see. His watch, the gold band on his ring finger, the tiny hair curling at his wrists, his eyes warm and flecked with gold. Grays line his temple and his haircut is immaculate. The glasses suit him. As if aware of my eyes on him, he looks at me. I am tempted to look away but I hold his gaze.

He rises abruptly and asks. "Where are we going to eat?"

I am still seated. "By when do you have to be back?"

He looks at his watch. "I need to attend the session on IP rights and that is the last for the day at 4:00 pm. I'm all yours until then." I think I catch a smile in his eyes as he looks at me.

I get up and walk to the door. He follows and we walk to Reading Terminal. "So, how have you been?" he asks. I feel years of anger rise through my spine. I match his stride and turn to look at him, answering evenly. "Let's pick up some food and go somewhere we can talk." Catching the edge in my voice, he remains silent until we get sandwiches, a drink and find a cab to Rittenhouse Park. I have been here a couple of times with Vikram and lead us to the bench off the walking trail that is close to a pond. There are stragglers ambling around, but it is not crowded.

We sit, leaving a sizable gap between us. I take out the food, the drinks, and the napkins before I put my bag by my side. The brisk walk has made me warm and I shrug my jacket off. He has not taken his eyes off me.

"I have been well, thank you," I say, answering the question he had asked half an hour ago. "And you?" I add as an afterthought. He takes a bite of his sandwich and chews slowly before answering. "I've been better."

We eat mostly in silence, parrying the talk that is to come with safe questions and answers.

"How is Ashwin doing? Where is he these days?" I ask

"Ashwin is in Atlanta. He works for a medical accessories company. Married with two kids. He married his school classmate, Sneha. She works from home as a social media marketer. My parents' shuttle between Madras and Atlanta every year. They land at Austin and stay for a week and come back again for a week before they fly out. At least he is propagating the family name," he says wryly.

"What about your sister, Usha?" he asks I am surprised he remembers her name.

"She is good. She works for Google. Settled in the Bay area. She married her classmate, Aravind. They have a son, Ishaan. Like yours, my parents' shuttle between India and the two coasts too."

I take another bite, chew, and swallow. Suddenly I cannot bear to dance around the past anymore.

"How do you know Anand?" I ask abruptly. He blinks and understanding registers in his eyes. "He is my cousin from Coimbatore."

Now I go straight for the jugular. I pull out the book mark, the steel burnished and bright under the sunlight. The engraving standing out in relief as I hold it out. He reaches for it and flinches when I pull it back.

"Why did you walk away? I have the bookmark you left behind. I know you were there, Aditya," I state simply.

The question lies between us, shimmering in the afternoon sun. The seconds that tick by seem ominous. I see him open and close his mouth a couple of times as if composing and deleting answers. I cross my arms across my chest and wait.

"I don't know," he says and his voice drops as if he is unsure about what he wants to say next.

I feel like screaming but force myself to stay quiet and look at my hands instead.

"Sandhya, I must start at the beginning. Will you be patient? I have had fourteen years to wonder about it."

I look up at him and see raw pain etched on his face. I am not sure if I am surprised or not. Suddenly, I do not want to know. I consider grabbing my bag and walking away. As if sensing my thoughts, he reaches for my hand.

I shrug his hand away.

———

ADITYA: MEAT OF THE MATTER

I look at her sitting across from me. My hand smarts from the rejection, but I know I deserve it. I feel a longing for everything that could have been but is not. I take a deep breath and start.

"Remember that first day at school in eighth grade, when you and I were the only new students that year? I saw your braided hair, the glasses, and the earnestness with which you answered questions and I felt like we could be friends. The first few days, I sat next to Karthik. For some reason he had decided I was his friend. We ate lunch together and soon he had me clued into what brought on teasing by other guys. My accent and lapsing into 'Northie' Tamil were one. Books, I learned, were for pansies. On the one hand I wanted to fit in, be a part of the popular crowd. On the other, I just wanted to be left alone.

"In English classes, you raised your hand too often to count. The boys called you "Mary." I am not sure if you were even aware of that. I was envious of your ability to be yourself. When you wrote, you poured yourself into it. Your words spoke to me more than any friend I have had. I do not know how you saw yourself. To me, you were beautiful."

I pause and notice she is listening. I also realize that I had never acknowledged what I had just told her even to myself. She tucks her hair behind her ears. A gesture that brings on a new flood of memories.

"I know the boys called me maami and auntie," she whispers.

I shift uncomfortably and continue.

"I was shallow. To be friends with you would mean I would be teased mercilessly. I went with the flow, pretending to ignore you in class. I would haunt the library just to see you. I started to read because I had to have a reason to be there. Over time, as I checked out the books you returned, what had started as a way to see you took over my life. I fell in love. With books. With words and with you."

I look up and see a smile playing on her lips.

"After school, when I found you and I were headed to Karuna, I could not believe my luck. I thought we could be friends and eventually more than friends. But I realized soon that nothing had changed.

"The first few months in the hostel were brutal. If any of the seniors caught us freshers talking to girls, we were thrashed mercilessly. Not that we were not beaten even otherwise. I got a reprieve from some unspeakable things because of Vetri's uncle, but the nights were tough. They would ambush us, drop sacks over our heads. hold our hands and legs back and punch us. I would black out and then wake with my whole body in pain.

"Some days, I would wake up in a strange room, wearing only my underwear and with no idea how I had got there. I was forced to drink. Initially I did it because I did not have a choice. Later, I drank because it made the pain bearable.

If I had considered that going to Karuna meant I could get to know you better, I gave up on the idea. The first year at college was hell. By the end of the year, the seniors welcomed us into their fold with a bizarre ceremony and I was then part of the club that perpetuated the same things on the incoming freshmen. I did what I could to help the freshers. Yet, it was not enough."

I am afraid to look up so I take a deep breath and continue.

"By the time we were in the second year, you had your group. I could not find you alone, ever. I frequented the library again, but this time, it was to escape the mindless talk among my hostel mates of girls, porn and sex. I hated it, but never found the courage to walk away from the gang.

"I do not know, Sandhya. I have looked back many times and all I can say is I have no excuse for why I did not walk away from people like Vetri and Rajesh and seek out groups who were more to my taste. I liked the clout Vetri wielded. It was as though in his shadow, I could be invisible and sometimes invincible. It was like I could do no wrong."

I notice the dull dirt laden slush on the grass as I talk. I find it easier to talk if I am not looking at her.

"The professors were liberal with their grades for us. We got question papers before the exams. We heard the results before the class did. It was like being part of a hallowed circle. I knew it was wrong yet, if it were not me with them, it would have been some other boy in class. I quelled whatever misgivings I had and used the group to my advantage. Trust me, I paid for it in the end.

"Somewhere in the third year, I started noticing you even more. It seemed like you never went anywhere without Surya. I hated the sight of him. I made sure I was never around where I could see you or him. Then things changed in the last year when we took math classes together.

Each time I saw you with a book, I would be tempted to talk to you and eventually I thought we had fallen into a friendship. I never worked up the courage to ask if you were seeing Surya. I just assumed you were."

I look up and she says nothing. So I continue.

"The last day of college, I was journalling in the stadium after I gave you the book. I saw you and your friends pass each other your yearbooks and laugh. I was envious of you. I watched until you left and then decided to pack and head for the station. I must have gone a good bit when I heard your scream. I froze. I wanted to move but could not. It was the worst moment of my life. I looked around, trying to find where you were and ran in the darkness without an idea of where I was going. I wasted precious time trying to find someone to go get help.

I stumbled, but saw a group on the ground a little way from me. When I got there, I could not believe what I was seeing."

My voice breaks, the intensity of the images in my head too much to talk about. She looks at me intently as if to urge me to continue.

"I pulled some of them away and pushed Rajesh off you. I am not sure if it was the sight of me that stopped them or the sirens of the campus police, but they took off. I covered you the best I could and asked someone to hunt Surya down and ask him to come."

Her voice interrupts me.

"Was I raped?"

I turn the question over in my head. I hesitate, close my eyes, and say, "Yes, I think so. I think you were. I do not know exactly what they did to you. When I found you, your clothes were torn, your eyes were closed and you were bleeding. But I think they had raped you."

We sit in silence as she takes it all in. Then I continue.

"Surya came in a few minutes. He managed to get an ambulance and told me he was taking you to G.K.N.M. hospital where his aunt worked. The last I saw you; you were being loaded onto a stretcher. That was the moment I knew that what I felt for you could not hold a candle to Surya's feelings for you. He looked like he was dead. At the same time, there was a rage inside him that radiated heat."

I look up and she is looking at the ground, her face impassive. So I go on.

"Later that night, Surya called me to ask a favor. He asked me to get Vetri to the old bus stop. He also asked me to make sure that I was seen with people Vetri knew. I did what he asked. I had no idea of what was being planned, but I did it. Later I heard Vetri had two of his fingers ripped off."

I look up and she is looking at me with something between fear and hunger. Her eyes are alight with a strange greed. I have no idea what is running through her mind, but talking about this feels cathartic to me. I have held this in for so many years that letting it out feels like blessed relief. I consider leaving out the shameful part I played in this story, but plough on, the confessional feeling strangely good.

"Because I was the only witness, I was summoned to the principal's office. You know he was Vetri's maama (uncle), right?" She nods. "They gave me an ultimatum. I keep silent or they would destroy my future. I had my admission for Drexel. Vetri had transferred money to my account weeks earlier to help me with my visa."

I pause, unable to look at her.

"I did nothing, Sandhya. I walked away. I walked away without checking if you wanted to file a complaint. I do not know if therapists have a name for this, but since then, I have had a sense of self-loathing that has destroyed me. I could never believe it if someone said they trusted me or loved me. I could never see myself worthy of any positive feeling. I have suffered and I am suffering.

"I met Shankar last week. He told me that Vetri and Rajesh had both been castrated in addition to having their fingers chopped off. They are single and live here in the US. Seattle." I look up now, my eyes swimming with tears. I see pain in hers.

"I have always loved you, Sandhya," I say.

"No!" Sandhya's voice is harsh.

I jerk, startled.

"No!" she says.

She stands up, her body shaking. I look at her, shocked.

"No, Aditya. You loved the idea of me. You loved the idea of a future with me. But if you truly cared for me, you would have stayed. You would have reached out. You wouldn't have disappeared without a trace."

I sink back against the bench as her face contorts with rage.

"If you loved me, you would have come to me, Aditya," she says. "You would have given me the closure I so desperately prayed for. But you have always walked away. You have always loved no one but yourself."

She stops and takes a deep breath. I am shaking now. I have never seen Sandhya so angry before. She radiates hate. I open my mouth to speak, but she gets in first.

"You selfish asshole!" she shouts. "Do you have any idea what it has been like for me? Don't bother to reply because no one can imagine the agony of being told that nothing has happened to you when your body screams with every cell that you have been damaged, that you have been ravaged, pilloried, plundered by animals.

"Do you know what it is like when you wake up with blood and injuries all over you, not knowing what happened to you or who did it to you?"

I gaze at her numbly. How had it never occurred to me how badly she could have been affected by it?

"Do you know what it is like to inspect the clothes you were wearing a few hours ago and finding them ripped and shredded? Do you know what it is like to look at yourself in the mirror and see scars and wonder whose hands roamed over you? Do you have any idea of how many times I showered in the days that followed, scrubbing myself raw because of how unclean I felt? Do you know how much I fear the darkness? Do you know I sill hate crowds, that I feel closed in and I cannot breathe."

She is sobbing helplessly by this time. It appears she'll never stop. I do not know what to do.

"Did you know that eventually Surya told me that he covered up the rape because it was for my best? That he had done it because he did not want my name dragged through mud? He did it to save my reputation, he said."

She laughs mirthlessly. I am too shaken to say anything in response.

"That evening before leaving Coimbatore, I had planned to ask him if he liked me enough to consider marrying me. I knew I liked him and that he liked me. I was sure he would have followed me to the ends of the earth if I had asked him."

" Instead that was the last time I saw him."

"I had nightmares for the longest time. I still do. I wake up screaming, suffocated, and gasping for air. I am not sure where I am until I see Vikram."

She stops, gulping for air. Her voice is quieter when she continues but it is as if she cannot control herself any longer.

"I could not let another person touch me without panicking. I drove away every suitor I had by the compulsive sharing of my history. I wanted to scare them away. And I did. Do you know how much my parents suffered with me?"

"Every day for the first few years, I prayed to God that Vetri and Rajesh would die a violent, painful death. It took years of therapy to try and forget even if not forgive. Even now, sometimes I wonder if they married. If their families know the vile kind of people they are."

She pauses, spent. "Do you know after I was married, I could not bear to have sex with my husband because a part of me was so damaged that I could not bear intimacy of any kind? Do you know the amount of therapy I have had and yet I still have nightmares and I wake up sometimes screaming your name?"

"No, Aditya, you did not love me. No one did, until Vikram. He held me while I wept and sobbed. He held back his frustration while he helped me heal. But you know what, even love is not enough. The trauma of what I went through, the not knowing, the feeling of being violated, over and over in my head. The knowledge that the guys who did this to me did so because they thought I was your girlfriend, the knowledge that this vile thing happened to me just because I was in the wrong place at the wrong time..."

She trails off. I cannot bring myself to speak.

"I thought when I finally I knew what happened, I could find closure," she says. "But I feel no joy, no vindication, nothing."

She shakes her head and picks up her bag.

"I wish you well, Aditya. I must go now."

———

SANDYA: LETTING GO OF THE PAST

I walk away in a haze of anger, my legs carrying me purely by force of habit. I pause to collect where I am and call a cab. I text Vikram, telling him I am heading home.

The cab jolts through the evening traffic, stopping and starting, stopping, and starting. I feel numb. The inside of the cab feels suffocating. I want to cry but my eyes feel dry. The air around me is arid, cracking under the weight of everything I have heard. I laugh morosely at the idea of Aditya having been in love with me.

What is love? Had I been in love with him? Do shared experiences count as love?

I think of Vikram, my Vik, who patiently waited for me to be okay with intercourse, setting aside his frustrations and talking to me about it when I was in the frame of mind to understand what it was like from his side. Our ability to talk through every situation has gotten us through the best and the worst of our lives. If that is not love, what is?

It feels surreal to know exactly what had happened to me after so many years. Pages from the report from the hospital swim before my eyes. The voice of the principal echoes, "Not a rape case." The injustice of it all wants me to curl up into a ball and cry. Yet, I am sitting, motionless, in a cab hurtling away from the man who could have stayed and helped me make sense of what had happened, but did not.

I feel a cold anger flare up inside me, this time against Surya.

I think of him and Vennila, married, probably with children, going on with their lives after having decided what was best for me. A bitterness engulfs me for all that could have been. All that has been. The not knowing had consumed me. The knowing seems to do little either. I am still the same Sandhya. The girl who was raped. The girl who carries with her the trauma of violence. The girl who is now struggling with being unable to become a mother.

What had I imagined the truth would do? Set me free? Return me whole, untouched, unblemished. I let out a wild laugh and the cab driver looks at me through the mirror. There is concern in his eyes. I avert my eyes and look down.

Soon, I am on the train speeding back to Malvern, back home, amid a crush of bodies all going back to their lives. I look around me and wonder how many women harbor dark secrets like I do. They all look haggard, weighed down by their lives.

I feel tired. A tiredness that is bone deep.

Vikram is at the station, much to my surprise. He holds me wordlessly. I hand him my car keys and he says we can get my car the next day. He settles me in the passenger seat of his pickup and we drive home in silence. I am too spent to tell him what had happened. Strangely, there seems to be no need to. He seems to intuit that I cannot now.

We reach home and I head for the shower. I let the hot water wash over me. I scrub myself raw. The tears come finally, mingling with the soap and water, and get washed away. I scream, a raw primal sound. I see Vikram rush to the door. He stays, letting me process my grief the only way I know.

He holds me, drying me and wrapping me in a warm towel. He dresses me the way one would a child. I seem to have frozen both in my body and my mind. He puts me to bed, tucks me in and settles down in the chair with the nightlamp on, watching me fall into a deep dreamless sleep.

———

ADITYA: UNTANGLING MESSY LIVES

I watch, stunned as Sandhya walks unsteadily into the fading light. My mind is unable to process anything she had said. I stay rooted, the cold seeping into my body. After what feels like hours, I manage to pull myself up, put my gloved hands into my pockets and walk aimlessly.

"…You have always walked away, Aditya. You have always loved only yourself…"

"… you selfish asshole…"

Sandhya's words echo in my head. I feel angry. She had walked away before I could defend myself. I smart, the anger and guilt pulsing in my head.

My phone buzzes and I ignore it.

"…You have always walked away, Aditya. You have always loved only yourself… you selfish asshole…"

The irony is not lost on me. I have walked away, haven't I? From everything that mattered. I had never once taken a stand, made a statement or even taken a hard look at situations where I'd felt I was the victim.

The phone buzzes again. I pull it out and Rashmi's voicemail is loud.

"Where are you, Aditya? Should we wait for you or will you meet us at the restaurant?"

I call Rashmi back, apologize and say something about the meeting running over. I ask them to head to the restaurant and I would join them when I am done.

I hail a cab and stop to grab my laptop from the office. I watch the meter tick as we leave the city and head towards Wayne. I settle in for the forty-minute ride and feel blank.

Sandhya had been right.

As I peer out in the darkness, visions of the past few months with Uma play out in my head in montages. I feel a stirring of shame. I had been so fixated on seeing how she could fit into my life and how she could meet me halfway that I'd lost sight of the fact that I had not moved at all. While I had rued her lack of interest in world affairs and the written word as a failing, I had missed out on everything else about her.

Meeting Sandhya seems to have freed me of the image I had carried in my head of the perfect woman for me. The depth of her rage and the intensity of the hatred she carried for me had had me smarting. I had been an asshole. I still was one. Had my actions been self-preservation or selfishness? I no longer know or care. All I know is that the past must be left behind. The past has kept me moored in one place for so long that I seem to have lost my way.

The cab slows and I snap out of my reverie. I direct the driver to the restaurant where the rest are waiting for me. I wave to them and head straight to the washroom. Splashing cold water on my face, I realize I have a lot of decisions to make.

"I am sorry I am late," I say and Anand waves me into a chair .

"You could have called, you know that, right? Uma was really looking forward to going out for dinner with you," Rashmi says from across me, her smile masking her irritation.

Uma looks rather fetching in the emerald green dress she is wearing.

"I am sorry," I say simply. She shrugs, used to my vagaries by now. "Uma, I am sorry. If you are still up to it, can we go for a drive after dinner? There are things I need to talk to you about."

I am not sure if she can read the repentance in my voice or if she is too tired to care. But she nods and scans the menu. We eat mostly in silence, Uma and I. Rashmi and Vibha are animated. I notice Anand watching us curiously. He averts his eyes when I look up.

I pay when we are done and we head home. Uma asks for a few minutes to refresh herself before our drive.

I watch Uma as she buckles herself in. Without makeup, she looks young and vulnerable. I am tempted to reach out and take her hand. I desist. We drive down Rt 30 and find an open bistro. We walk in and take a booth. There is no one else in the restaurant. I walk up to the counter and pay for two ice cream cones and a bottle of water.

She is silent, peering out the window into the parking lot.

"Uma."

She turns to look at me.

"I have a lot to talk to you about."

I start from the beginning. Over the sounds of the cars on the highway, I tell her about Sandhya, about Vetri, about my part in the story. I tell her about my lonely years in the US. I tell her about my fears and panic attacks. I leave nothing out.

She listens in silence, not interrupting, not taking her eyes off my face.

After I finish my account of lunch with Sandhya and why I am late, she reaches for my hand and takes it.

"Why are you telling me all this today?" The question seems incongruent. I consider asking her to repeat it and then think it over.

"I do not know, Uma. Sandhya said something today that hit home. She said I have never loved anyone but myself. I was angry when she said it. I felt defensive. I walked around, turning over what she said, and I realized it is true. I have always run away from problems. I have been so fixated on what I want, how my life should be, that there has been no place for anyone else. I should not have married you, especially when I was battling demons inside me."

I pause and look at our joined hands.

"I am sorry, Uma, I am truly sorry."

She does not say anything for a while. So I tell her about the offer the CIO had made me. I ask what she thinks. "It's your job, your decision," she says noncommittally.

Before I can press her for an answer, she starts speaking, slowly, softly.

"Aditya, I was in love with you for years before we got married. After we moved to Austin, I could not understand your behavior. I tried asking you but never really got any answers. So, I gave up after a while. Of late, I have been wondering why I am putting up with so much crap.

"I have been thinking about a separation. While all that you told me today helps me understand why you are the kind of person you are, it does not explain to me the reason behind your coldness. It does not explain to me how you could marry someone in good faith and treat them so apathetically. Fighting demons does not mean you have to be unkind to people around you, you know?"

She stops as if the discussion is pointless.

"I have thought about divorce on and off, but never really brought it out in the open. Do you know why, Aditya?"

Before I can attempt to say anything, she continues, "I could not answer the question 'why.' I have not been physically abused. You have always provided for me. You have done everything you should have done even though it has been clinical. Does indifference and apathy count as abuse? I am not sure."

She stops, withdraws her hand from mine.

"I need time, Aditya. I am willing to give us, this marriage, another chance. But I also think a short separation will give us perspective."

I look at her, my perspective of her changing. I nod. Words seem unnecessary. The path to redemption looks long and hard. I tell myself I will deal with this another day.

As we walk out of the restaurant, I reach for her hand . She does not resist.

"I will accept the offer to move here. You can stay with your cousins until you decide what you want to do. I want to make this marriage work, Uma. I am willing to put in the work. I am sorry for the past."

She says nothing.

"Are you guys okay?" Rashmi and Anand ask in unison as we enter

We both say, "Great" too quickly. We settle down on the sofa and catch up. I tell Anand and Rashmi about the meeting with the CIO and they are excited about the prospect of us moving here. Our conversation meanders to Sandhya and there is a moment when it dawns on all of us that she was connected to all of us in some way. The fact that she would be at the party makes it feel weird.

Uma prods and Rashmi opens up.

" It is more than that, Uma. We were good friends." She pauses and then continues.

"Sandhya and I were friends once. We had moved to the development we were in then around the same time. We were working in the same corporate park. We both did not have children. We spent a lot of time together and got to know each other well. Now, that I think of it, she never mentioned her college or where she went to school. She always talked about Bangalore and her working days there.

She was like the sister I never had. We went through infertility together. We scheduled appointments so we could support each other. Things changed when I got pregnant with Vibha and she miscarried. Watching my pregnancy was a reminder of what she missed out on. The worst part is that I knew how it felt. I had been there once too often. We could never really bridge the gap and when we moved out of the development, the friendship died a natural death. I think of her often and wonder what it would be like if we had started our families at the same time. We probably would still have been friends."

She trailed off into a wistful silence.

"I called her and Vikram on an impulse to our get-together tomorrow. She agreed to come."

The silence that falls seems to encompass the rest of the evening and I go to bed feeling curiously lighter and fall into a deep sleep.

HOLIDAY GET-TOGETHER

Uma wakes to the sun coming in through the window near her side of the bed. Aditya, surprisingly, is fast asleep.

Since she had stopped waking early to make his breakfast and lunch, he had been the one to rise first. He looked vulnerable almost, the mask he usually wore invisible. Their conversation from the night before plays in her head. She is wary. They have nothing to lose, really. She had already been mulling a break of sorts, but she is willing to give him another chance if he is truly willing to work for it.

The thoughts buzzing in her head beg to be set free. The blog seems too public for the kind of things she wants to write about. She pulls out the journal she carries in her bag. The one she writes in rarely.

~~~~~~~~~~~~~

It's Christmas Eve. Even as the world around me prepares to indulge in gift giving and starting anew with the New Year, I feel like I have hit a pause in my life. I have answers. Oh! I have answers that I had not bargained for. Knowing what I know now, I feel as conflicted as ever.

I know Aditya and I are headed for a separation. Permanent or temporary is something only time can tell. I can't wrap my head around the fact that guy I am married to walked away from a broken, battered, brutalized woman. He walked away. He walked away and did not turn back.

Do people change? Does the core of a person change? Am I willing to bet on this person who walked away? Do I want to?

The truth is I want to. I am tired of this life. I am going to start afresh. I am going to give us time and distance. I truly want him to walk the path to redemption and a part of me hopes he will. If he doesn't then I will have my answer.

It is not exactly the resolution I had hoped for, but I am certainly feeling relieved about no longer having to second guess and wonder what shadow I am living under.

I am going to put all this away for now, enjoy the rest of the break for what it is and start anew in every way when I am back in Austin.

She showers and changes into a pair of old PJs, knowing there is a lot to do around the house in anticipation of the party in the evening. She likes Rashmi and Anand. It is also nice to have a child in the house. Vibha is articulate and has been more than willing to let Uma paint her nails and talk shop with her.

Sandhya.

She must admit she is curious to meet the girl who had haunted most of Aditya's life. She had asked to see pictures of her but Aditya had none. She would have to wait to see.

The day passes with everyone helping. Aditya volunteers for a last-minute grocery run and to pick up the food from the caterer. Uma helps Vibha get ready and Anand and Rashmi go about dusting, setting corners straight, nudging off-center wall decor into place and lighting LED candles all over the house. It is amazing how a few well-placed candles bring with them a holiday vibe. The front door boasts a wreath of sorts that Vibha had made at school. The driveway is clear and they have blinking snowmen and reindeer set on the porch.

The first of the guests arrives at 6:00 pm. Rashmi and Anand are gracious hosts and Uma finds herself surrounded by people who are warm and happy to include her in their groups. She flits from group to group, introducing herself and Aditya. Aditya sticks near Anand, reluctant to circulate. He nurses a can of beer and watches Uma laugh and smile. The navy-blue sweater dress she had picked out for the evening becomes her, he thinks. It feels like he is really noticing her for the first time.

He feels a pull on his arm and turns to see Sandhya with a platter of cookies.

"Hi! Where do I leave these?"

He offers to take the platter from her and sets it down on the dessert table. Sandhya introduces him to Vikram and the men size up each other. Vikram is about his height, stocky and easy mannered. Vikram's eyes are piercing, making him uncomfortable. He shifts his weight and offers to introduce him to the rest of the folks he knows. Sandhya spies Rashmi and envelopes her in a hug.

Vikram holds on to Aditya's arm before he can move towards Anand.

"Aditya, I want to thank you," he begins. Aditya indicates for him to stop and leads him out to the patio. It is cold, but they can talk without being overheard.

"I want to thank you," Vikram says again. Aditya weighs what he wants to say in return.

"I am sorry I walked away from her... Actually, I am sorry for a whole lot of things. We have all borne the brunt of what happened in our own ways."

He is not sure why he is apologizing to Vikram, but it feels like the right thing to do.

"I cannot speak for what you should or should not have done. I am just thankful to you for giving Sandhya the pieces she needed to fill the gaps in her story. There is a lot of healing and grieving to do, but at this point all I can do is to give her space and be there to hold her when she falls," Vikram says.

Rashmi, Uma, and Sandhya are standing in a group near the stove. Vibha runs up to them and says, "Uma auntie is so cool! She has a beautiful green and gold butterfly tattoo on her shoulder. Amma, can I get a tattoo when I am older?"

Sandhya looks at Uma. Something clicks. TheSunGoddess's posts suddenly make sense. She looks around for Aditya, the Mister. She feels an overwhelming sense of loss on Uma's behalf.

"Rashmi, is it okay if I grab Uma and find a quiet place to talk? Can you handle things in the kitchen alone for a while?"

Rashmi nods, indicating the stairs. They can go upstairs where it is quieter and they are not likely to be disturbed, she says.

Uma leads Sandhya to her room. They stand there awkwardly. Sandhya breaks the silence. "I read your blog. I am a fan of yours. I have often left comments as the bookishdiva…"

Uma's eyes grow wide.

"I have a confession to make. I stumbled on Aditya's diaries earlier this week when I was looking for suitcases to pack. I read them. I know he was in love with you. I have no idea if you felt that way about him," Uma says in return.

There's silence after the two confessions. Then slowly, both women begin to smile.

"Our lives are a mess, aren't they?" Uma chuckles.

Sandhya instinctively reaches out and envelops Uma in a tight hug.

"Yes, they are. But we will heal too. At least I hope so. Does Aditya know about your blog?"

"No. I think I will shut it down. It has served its purpose. We had a talk last night. He told me what had happened. I told him how I felt. We are going to try separation for a while to see if that gives us perspective. I think it will. He needs to figure out what he wants from this relationship and so do I. But we are willing to give it another shot. Wish us luck," Uma says.

They head downstairs and join the rest of the group. The house is filled with holiday cheer. Sandhya notices Aditya watching her and walks toward him. They find a quiet corner. The silence is oppressive.

"I am sorry, Aditya says. "You were right, Sandhya. I have been a selfish asshole. I hurt you and I have hurt my wife. I only hope I can redeem myself for Uma."

Aditya looks wistful, his eyes seeking Uma in the crowd.

"You could try writing, you know? Uma is a wonderful writer. Her blogs kept me sane when I needed a place that felt joyous and bright. Usha and I are huge fans of her work," Sandhya says.

Aditya looks stunned. "She writes?"

"Yup! And writes well too."

Sandhya takes a sip of her drink. She looks at Aditya, the expression on her face a mix of pain and acceptance.

"About yesterday," she says, fiddling with the stem of her wineglass. "I want to let you know that it will be a while for me to process everything you told me. I have no idea if I want to be in touch with you or even have you in my life again. If anything brings me back into your life, it might be Uma."

She sets her glass down on a table.

"Now, go, find your wife and stick with her," Sandhya says. "She is new to this place and there is nothing more lonesome than navigating a space full of people you don't know."

With that, Sandhya picks up her glass again and walks away, searching for Vikram. The rest of the evening is filled with lots of food and conversation. Sandhya and Vikram leave a little before midnight and Uma hurries to click a selfie with them before they leave.

When the house empties and Vibha is in bed, the four adults clean up and Aditya knows in his heart that his decision to move will be good for him. He looks at Uma and hopes she will feel that way too. They exchange tired good nights as they head to their respective rooms.

Uma looks at all the pictures she had clicked on her phone over the course of the evening. Aditya is already asleep. She uploads them to Facebook with the caption "Thankful for a new beginning" and tags Aditya.

Across the globe, Vennila is online. Her feed refreshes with a notification that says Anita liked Aditya's picture. She does a double take when the picture turns out to be one of Aditya and possibly his wife Uma. She clicks on the pictures Aditya is tagged in and sees Sandhya leaning against a handsome man. She calls Surya.

"Surya, you have to come see this."

Surya walks up, putting on his glasses, and peers over her shoulder. He draws a deep breath as he looks at the picture. They gaze at the picture. Sandhya is smiling. Her eyes sparkle. A sense of guilt that they did not know they had been holding on to finds release. Vennila and Surya look at each other. Surya's hands press on her shoulder and Vennila squeezes his hand back.

Vennila clicks through to Sandhya's profile and sends a friend request.

———

SANDHYA: MOVING ON

I wake up to the sunlight filtering in through the honeycomb blinds. I am surprised to find Vikram's arms enclosing me, the warmth from his body inviting me to snuggle in. I trace the profile of his face. He smiles in his sleep.

I gently move his arms away and step into the bathroom. The clock reads 5:30 am. I am up early for a Sunday. I sip my coffee in the sun room, watching the frost melt under the rays of the sun. I am filled with something that feels ebullient. I want to call it hope. When something has been haunting you for so long that it becomes part of your psyche, you almost feel it physically.

I look back on my life, the years of struggle following college, the anger and resentment that found its outlet in the close-knit circle around me. I think of Amma. I am taken back to the weekends she would show up in Bangalore, Appa in tow, wanting to touch me, hold me physically, assure herself that I was all right. I had acted for them, pretending all was well, until the screams at night had told them otherwise. They had wanted to move to Bangalore to help staunch my fears. I had refused. I wonder how they had spent those years before Vikram promised them he would try and heal me.

I think of Vikram, our struggles with intimacy and our struggles with infertility. I think of how he has gone on gamely, never once mentioning that he wished things were different. I think of Vibha. I think of what could have been. I have been so focused on what I have lost that I have not accounted for what I have, what he wants.

The coffee has cooled. I set it down and lower myself to the floor, leaning against the cool glass. I love the interplay of light as it slants inside. The leaves of the Tulsi plant are curling. I make a mental note to water it.

The sun rises in a glorious explosion of light. Inexplicably, my thought turns towards Surya. I wonder where he is. I wonder if he married Vennila. The anger I had felt towards them has been replaced by nothingness. It is a dull ache, nothing more.

I think about what Aditya had told me. I try and imagine Surya looking at me as I lay bleeding. I wonder if he punched Vetri and Rajesh till he was spent. I feel a shudder go through me as I imagine Vetri and Rajesh lying unconscious, their manhood being stripped away. My burning need for revenge had long passed. I had told myself that I could never forgive them, but now I know that they have been forced to live with the consequences of their actions every day. I wonder who did the act, the surgical knife slicing through skin. Did he or she do it out of obligation to Surya? Was Surya any different from Vetri in that sense, wielding a God-like power over someone vulnerable? I shake my head, wondering what causes people to act like they do even in the face of societal pressures.

I get up, feeling cold even with the sun washing over me. With nothing much to do, I decide to go for a run around the neighborhood. Slipping into comfortable pants and an active tee, I dig out a matching jacket, lace up my shoes and head out. The temperature is in the forties and I know I will warm up in a bit. I stretch before I start and jog slowly, savoring the quiet and peace of the morning. I pass a couple of people out with their dogs. I wave and keep moving. My mind wanders to the day before. The combination of relief and exhaustion is too much and I shelve the processing I will have to do after Aditya's revelations.

For years I have wondered, what if I had not left the book behind? What if I had returned the stadium sooner or later? These exercises have been futile, leaving me only with the anguish of 'why me?' I have wondered if the same fate would have taken any girl who had wandered that way or if it had happened that way because it had been me. Some questions have no answers.

I think of Uma, of Uma and Aditya. I hope he has the sense to hold on to her. She has a sense of irrepressible energy about her that Aditya could do with.

Strangely, I do not miss Vennila. Perhaps because we had banded together out of need and then stuck together because of Surya. I imagine she is married to a businessman, that diamonds wink in her ears, that she manages a busy household. Images of Surya and Vennila together come to me unbidden.

My thoughts veer toward Surya again. I wonder about the path his life has taken. Does he think of me? Is he happy? Does he have children? I imagine a child with Surya's curly hair and kind eyes and feel a pang. The images I carry in my head of our times together fade, become sepia toned. I realize I only remember the good times. The easy laughter, the early morning conversations about dreams and aspiration, the endless food, the car rides, the sentimental notes, the gifts. The unspoken promises. The lines blurring between friendship and love. I feel an ache for what could have been. For a moment I wish with my heart that he has found happiness.

I have run further than I usually do and find myself in the neighboring development. I turn and jog toward home. The sun is higher now and the homes on either side of the road are slowly waking up. Cars slow down as they pass me. With each step I take towards home, I feel lighter. The ghosts of the past are evaporating with the morning sun.

I let myself in to see Vikram at the kitchen, brewing coffee. We take our mugs and sit in the patio, watching the world around us wake up.

———

ADITYA - UMA: NEW BEGINNINGS

Aditya and I reach Austin late at night. He heads to bed after a shower while I let the hot water wash over me, feeling cleansed and happy. Instead of turning in for the night, I unpack the suitcases, putting away clothes to be laundered and unwrapping gifts that Rashmi had pressed into my hands as we left. I find a bunch of old pictures of Aditya and some temple jewelry. I am touched and put them away in my dresser.

My life as I know it seems to have come full circle. I call my mother to let her know I am back and that I had a good time. I think about calling my in-laws but decide that can wait until the morning. I miss my blog, but realize it has run its course.

I feel clearer in my head. I wonder if I should let Aditya move to Philly and stay back for a while. I could stay here at our townhouse and explore other options. The distance will give me perspective and possibly give Aditya a chance to miss me. I feel lighter, knowing I have a plan of action.

Aditya stirs as I slip into bed. As I turn the lights out, he draws me to him and we sink into sleep together.

The next morning, Aditya tells me that he was going to let his CIO know that he is accepting the offer. He scans my face, looking for misgivings of any sort.

"Good luck, Aditya! I know you will do well," I tell him. I pause and continue, having mulled over it at night.

"I am not sure what timeframe you are looking at for the move, but I have a request. Can we keep this townhouse for a little while longer?"

He looks at me perplexed. "I was thinking of letting Tim know that I can start in Philly by February. Why?"

"Perfect. You go on, find an apartment near the city. I will stay here until spring, list the house and figure out what to do with my life."

I see a trace of fear on his face and realize it makes me happy that he cares. Before he can say anything, I continue.

"I just want a break, Aditya. I tried my best to be a good wife, someone you would fall in love with eventually. I figured taking a break from work would help me focus on building a family with you. Here I am, five years later, with an empty shell of a marriage, no children, and no career. I know you say you will try, but I think this separation will help us both.

"I want to figure out what I want career-wise. I know I want a child but I want him or her to have parents who are in love with each other." I pause, emotions getting the better of me. Promising myself I will not break down, I turn away.

Aditya reaches for me, hesitating as he draws me into a hug as if considering my feelings for the first time. He lifts my chin so I can look into his eyes.

"Uma, I understand where you are coming from. I am okay with you staying back for a while. I also want you to know that I want this marriage to work. This time around, I will meet you halfway. Will you give me a second chance?"

I nod, unable to speak. He lets go of my arm and heads for the bathroom. An hour later, he is ready and offers to get donuts for breakfast. He lingers near the door as if turning over words inside his head. I think he means to say, "I love you," but it comes out as "I'll be back soon" instead.

I throw a round of laundry into the washer after he leaves and pull up a list of grad schools near Philadelphia. The phone rings. It is my mom-in-law. She reads out my fortune for the day from the papers. "Good fortune comes to those who wait," it says. I laugh. "Come, visit us," I tell her and she says she will. "I am waiting for good news from you, kannu."

I blush and change topics.

———

EPILOGUE: AND LIFE GOES ON
26 NOVEMBER, 2015

Somewhere on the highway in the dusky Thanksgiving night, two cars are headed to Wayne, PA. It is a charming neighborhood populated by the rich and the neo-rich. Smells of cooking emanate from the houses and mingle underneath starry skies. The air is cold and it smells like snow. At the driveway of 341, Warren Ct off Old Eagle School Road, tiny winking lights encircle the mailbox. Icicle lights dangle from the soffits. A lush mixture of laughter and bonhomie can be heard through the curtained windows. The table is set. Tofurkey has pride of place, cranberry bread and mashed potatoes speckled with chives next to it. A covered pot of fragrant biriyani is on the right. A pack of foil-covered warm naan sits next to the paneer. Pumpkin pie competes with warm kheer.

Somewhere overhead, Vibha stands in her new strapless blue dress, adjusting her earrings, and is pleased with the reflection staring back at her. Rashmi fusses with her long black dress and Anand lounges in his corduroys, refusing to 'dress up' as he calls it. It's just family, he says.

On Rt 202, Sandhya and Vikram are ensconced in their warm car, a casserole of lasagna warming Sandhya's lap. At work, she had requested a lateral move that had pre-empted her reporting to Aditya. Vikram is driving and they are wondering if they should share the news that they are paper pregnant. With the specter of the past only a faint outline,

Sandhya had broached the topic of adoption and found Vikram surprisingly hesitant. She had let it go, but over the past year, Vikram had come around.

"I am excited, Vik, but also scared of jinxing it. Also, we will need to talk to our families first." Sandhya says. Vikram looks at her, his calm eyes twinkling behind his round glasses. "What is meant to be will happen. Look back on our lives and you will see."

"O, Saint Vik. I bow to thee." Sandhya does a deep bowing gesture and they laugh. Indulgent laughs, reminiscent of an easy relationship. The ghosts of the past have floated away, leaving the promise of a radiant future.

Her phone pings with an incoming message. Vennila has sent a picture of Shyam playing cricket. Lanky and tall, his eyes remind her of Surya. She saves the picture and replies to Vennila.

On the Penna Turnpike, Aditya and Uma are driving in companionable silence. Love Story plays on the radio. Uma is humming along. Aditya is relaxed and enjoying the drive. He had walked the path to redemption and is basking in the glow of a love well earned. In the past three years, Uma has earned an MBA from the Fox Business School, found a job as digital strategy analyst in the city and fallen in love with Aditya afresh. She and Aditya have an easy friendship she cherishes and Sandhya, Rashmi and she meet up occasionally for drinks and dinner in town.

Aditya seems lost in thought. He has done well for himself in his new role. Perhaps it is the fact that he is turning forty or the fact that Ashwin and Sneha are expecting another child, but something seems to be been stirred up within him. For the first time in his life, he is longing for a life-long commitment, family, and kids. He turns to look at Uma and their eyes meet.

Somewhere over the horizon, Usha is working on an email trying to coax Sandhya into agreeing to let her be a surrogate for her. Ashwin and Sneha are planning a family reunion for the Christmas break.

In hindsight, the future is being scripted.

* * *

Acknowledgements

This book is possible because of the many people who have offered support from the time it was an idea in my head to its current form.

I owe a debt of gratitude to these people. Kushal Gulab my editor helped me keep the faith in this work even as my enthusiasm flagged, Santhya Shenbagam, my illustrator who brought my concept to life in the cover and, helped me get the book to a publish ready format.

My beta readers made a world of difference as the book made its way to its current form. So, a huge thank you to Akila Natarajan who spent hours on the phone discussing the plot and characters, Suman Murali who meticulously provided notes, Shymol James who made me feel like the best writer ever, Srividya Srinivasan who made me look at my work critically and, Lakshmi Gopal who was my first editor.

I would be amiss if I did not mention Lorraine Storms, my writer friend who provided moral support, held my hand through the publishing process and, cheered me on from start to finish.

My biggest cheerleaders are my family. I will forever be indebted to Amma, Kannan, Anjali, Meghna and, Sahana.

About the Author

Staring at the stars, decoding the teenage world of her kids and, working five days a week are ways Lakshmi spends her time. When she is not watching Korean or Chinese dramas, she is conjuring up worlds in her head that become her next book.

Lakshmi is the author of the children's book, "Why Is My Hair Curly?"

Lakshmi can be found online at

www.lgiyer.com